W9-CSN-174

PRAISE FOR HOLLY SCHINDLER'S *FERAL*

"Opening with back-to-back scenes of exquisitely imagined yet very real horror, Schindler's third YA novel hearkens to the uncompromising demands of her debut, *A Blue So Dark*. This time, the focus is on women's voices and the consequences they suffer for speaking. This is a story about reclaiming and healing, a process that is scary, imperfect, and carries no guarantees."

—*Publishers Weekly* (starred review)

"A heavily gloomy feel pervades this novel that shifts through phases of fantasy, mystery, psychological thriller, and thoughtful realistic fiction dealing with PTSD."

—ALA *Booklist*

"From the opening pages readers will be immediately immersed in this dark story, which has echoes of classic Hitchcock. Issues of cliques, peer pressure, bullying, self-esteem, post-traumatic stress syndrome, teacher-student relationships, and pet abandonment will provide substance for discussion."

—*School Library Journal*

"In the town of Peculiar, the cats aren't the only ones keeping secrets. . . . A dark and creepy psychological who-done-it that will keep you guessing until the very end."

—Jody Casella, author of *Thin Space*

"Wow! This book starts off with a bang—two of them, actually—and then it sinks its claws into you and never lets go."

—April Henry, *New York Times* bestselling author

spark

HOLLY SCHINDLER

HARPER TEEN

An Imprint of HarperCollinsPublishers

HarperTeen is an imprint of HarperCollins Publishers.

Spark

Copyright © 2016 by Holly Schindler
www.epicreads.com

Library of Congress Cataloging-in-Publication Data
Names: Schindler, Holly, date, author.
Title: Spark / Holly Schindler.
Description: First edition. | New York, NY : HarperTeen, an imprint of
    HarperCollinsPublishers, [2016] | Summary: "Quin is convinced
    the local theater is setting the stage for her two classmates to relive a
    romance from their town's past"— Provided by publisher.
Identifiers: LCCN 2015029172 | ISBN 9780062220233 (hardback)
Subjects: | CYAC: Theater—Fiction. | Love—Fiction. | Magic—Fiction.
    | Foundlings—Fiction. | Adoption—Fiction. | BISAC: JUVENILE
    FICTION / General. | JUVENILE FICTION / Horror & Ghost
    Stories. | JUVENILE FICTION / Social Issues / General (see also
    headings under Family).
Classification: LCC PZ7.S34634 Sp 2016 | DDC [Fic]—dc23 LC
    record available at http://lccn.loc.gov/2015029172

Typography by Kate J. Engbring
16 17 18 19 20   CG/RRDH   10 9 8 7 6 5 4 3 2 1

First Edition

All the world's a stage,
And all the men and women merely players.
—William Shakespeare, *As You Like It*

When I dream, it's always on a screen. And I'm always in the Avery Theater. And the Avery is always new—not the rotting, early-1900s building it is today. Every one of my dreams starts as I prop my sneakers into the balcony seat, hug my knees, and stare at the ornate gilded box seats, the brass faces of the theater. I get that dip in my stomach—the one that's like a horn blaring, announcing excitement is on its way. And I smile as the red velvet curtains part and the ancient projector pops to life.

In my most recurring dream, I see my mom, Dahlia, when she's a little girl. It's 1947, and she's bursting from the side exit of the Avery Theater, squealing in pain and fear as the nearby bushes grab her brown pigtails and yank her backward.

It makes total sense, really. Why wouldn't I dream about

this? It's been my bedtime story since I was in pigtails, too. Always the last thing I ever heard before falling asleep.

So it's this same scene, flashing across the screen of my mind: Dahlia's Mary Janes clicking as she races across the town square of Verona, Missouri. But she stops, her eyes wide, chest heaving, as she glances at the businesses that line the small town square. Few lights are still on, so late on that summer night. She whimpers because she knows no one will believe her, not about two bodies lying on a stage, not about Nick and Emma being hurt. "Oh, you silly little girl," they'll all say, rolling their eyes and scooting her back onto the sidewalk. "Trouble," everyone calls her, the eight-year-old busybody who's always barging into the florist or the hardware store or the barber's, telling whoppers and getting tangled up in shop-keepers' legs.

But tonight there *is* trouble. There's been a horrible fight inside the theater—and an accident. Involving Emma, the daughter of the Avery's owner; Emma, the very first female valedictorian of Verona High; Emma, who has college waiting for her; Emma, who has always been so kind to Dahlia, letting her have free Slo Pokes from the Avery concession stand. Emma's been hurt. Bad. And so has Emma's boyfriend, Nick, the out-of-town musician. Dahlia's afraid for Nick, too—even though he does call her Grace, after the smallest note in all of music, when Dahlia hates being reminded that she's small, powerless, just a little girl.

Dying, she thinks. *They might be dying.*

Dahlia glances up toward her mother's hat store. Her mother is one of the few still up, and she's changing the front-window display, putting out the new straw sun hats that recently arrived from California, special delivery.

But it would only take the mention of the Avery for her mother to frown and shout, "You slipped out of your room without permission to bother *George* again?" She won't believe that George, Emma's father, needs their help. She'll only get after Dahlia for telling another wild story. She'll be embarrassed that her little girl's causing trouble again.

Dahlia swallows the scream building up in her throat when she turns to see the only person in town who's never called her by that awful pet name. Who's never said, "Well, if it isn't Trouble," when she comes skipping past.

"Bertie." Dahlia breathes with relief, her feet attacking the pavement as she races to her side. "Help! Emma—Nick—they—" Dahlia jabs her trembling finger into the air, pointing toward the theater marquee that advertises, "TONIGHT! EMMA HASTINGS AS HOPE HARCOURT IN ANYTHING GOES!"

But Bertie's eyes are fixed on the sky beyond the theater, where the horizon burns a strange yellow-green—even though the sunset faded hours ago. Odd flames leap, forging a path through the stars. "The sky is talking to us, Dahlia," she whispers. "We're too far south to see the aurora borealis, so it can't be that. It's more. It's magic." At her side, the slender fingers of her right hand clutch the edge of the journal she always carries with her; its pages rustle in a sudden breeze, flipping back and forth.

"No! No more talking skies," Dahlia replies. "That stuff's bonkers. Nick and Emma—they need help." Disappointment makes her face droop. But she should have known, really. Bertie is a lot of things—she's eighteen, for starters. The same age as the two people dying on the Avery stage. She's also a kook—or so the entirety of Verona has proclaimed. Tragedy has scrambled her brains, poor thing, and now she walks the streets of town muttering gobbledygook about the skies talking. And magic.

Which means that mostly, Bertie is terrifying. Because it's easy to dismiss a crazy old woman. Wrinkles and white hair and an arthritic bend in the shoulders are easy to shrug away. But a crazy *young* woman, who is physically strong and can keep up with you if you try to run—she's terrifying. To everyone but Dahlia, anyway.

"Look how the stars are beginning to pop," Bertie instructs. "Do you see the shape they're taking? The stars are forming an X. It's a sign! I know it is." She flips through her journal, as though searching for a line that will help her decode the message in the sky.

Bertie was a writer, too—just like I am. Or maybe it's that we're secret writers. Nothing more than scribblers, actually. But why wouldn't we be so similar? Bertie, the biggest kook to have ever lived in Verona, Missouri, was my great-grandmother. Biological. And Dahlia, the little girl begging for help in the Verona square, the little girl who always had a soft spot for Bertie, is the one who adopted me.

Which is surely another reason why this dream keeps finding me. It makes me feel like we're all three a set of those nesting dolls—Dahlia a step larger than me, Bertie a step larger than Dahlia. All of us stacked one on top of each other. Me at the bottom.

Like it always does at this point in the dream, a siren wails, growing louder as a single red fire truck tears through the streets of Verona.

Headlights flash into Dahlia's eyes; the horn blares its warning.

Dahlia grabs Bertie's arm, tugging her backward, making her step out of the fire truck's path. The speeding truck kicks up enough wind to push Dahlia's pigtails back, dry out her eyes.

Shouts burst like firecrackers against the night as an emergency crew climbs from the fire truck, and as the front door of the Avery flies open.

"Don't tell me it's too late," Emma's father begs the firefighters. "It can't be."

"Did this happen on the stage?" Bertie gasps.

"Yes," Dahlia whispers.

Bertie frowns, concentrating. "The stage. And the way the stars are lined up to form that X . . ." She drops her journal, grabbing Dahlia by the shoulders. "Star-crossed lovers!

"A real-life Romeo and Juliet. Right here—in fair Verona! It's a play—it happened on the stage, just like this. You know the story, don't you? Everyone does. They were torn apart, Romeo and Juliet, by outside forces—their families didn't want them to be together. Just like George was afraid that Emma would run off with Nick! Yes! It's all the same, don't you see?"

Dahlia shrinks, pulling her arms free at the same moment that the Avery marquee throws electric sparks into the sky, higher even than the odd green flames. And then it goes dark. Beneath the green swirls in the sky, the front of the theater turns black. The bricks crackle like decaying autumn leaves. The building withers on fast forward. It instantly becomes dilapidated and ramshackle, with cracked windows and broken front steps and a torn awning. The gargoyles along the roof darken, and their faces disappear as though they've all been rubbed away by decades of rough weather.

"Did you see that?" Bertie whispers. "The Avery just died."

This, too, is nuts. Deep inside, all those years ago, Dahlia knew it. I've always known it, too—even when the grown-up Dahlia, who'd officially become "Mom," first started telling me this story, her voice rising and falling between her dramatic pauses. Even back when I first started having my dream. It's funny—I never did dream of Cinderella or princesses. But then, I never did get those kinds of bedtime stories. Maybe Mom, nearly retired by the time I was adopted, had a different idea about what was right to tell kids at night. A different idea about what made a great story. Maybe Cinderella bored her. But the square—and the Avery, which was at one time a living, breathing theater, a theater whose heart stopped beating the first time a true (and not play-pretend) tragedy unfolded on its stage—never did stop fascinating her.

Still, though, I knew it—even when I first heard the tale. I knew it was full of nonsense spouted long ago by a woman with scrambled brains. A dead building. A dead theater. Sure.

"But in the play, you know," Bertie tells little Dahlia, "Juliet took a drug, and was dead but not dead. She came back. The skies are talking to us, making a promise. Yes. This story isn't finished. It's not over. Don't you see?"

Bertie tilts Dahlia's chin so they can look each other square in the face. "Listen to me," she demands. "When the right hearts come to the Avery—at the right time—for the right reasons—this sky will return. The magic of the theater will return. The Avery will come back from the dead."

It's always at this point in the dream when I jerk myself awake, achy and sweaty. Like I do every single time without fail, I kick at the covers and grab my glasses from my nightstand. I pad across my bedroom floor, press my face against the window. And look up and down the square for any sign of magic.

After all, Dahlia and I still live where she has spent the entirety of her seventy-plus years, right here above the old hat store (which is no longer a hat store but a perfumery). We live on the opposite side of the square—directly across from the Avery Theater. In full view of any magic that just might want to show its quirky face.

I squint, inspecting the black brick and the rotten facade for some sign of life. For the aurora borealis to start swirling through the sky.

But the Avery is dead. As it has been dead since that fateful night back in 1947 when two star-crossed lovers really did die on the stage. When my mom really did witness the tragedy.

The sky is dark.

I shake my head. Who am I to expect something magical to happen for me? I'm the great-granddaughter of the biggest kook to have ever walked the streets of Verona, Missouri. I'm a B-average student with big glasses and plain hair. Magic is for girls who have far flashier backgrounds and powers and look like drawings of superheroes in comic books.

At least, that's what I've always believed. That's the kind of thing I always wind up telling myself after one of these dreams.

But right here, at the beginning of it all, I have no idea how wrong I am about that.

two

In Verona High's room 235, Advanced Drama is the catch-can for the senior nobodies.

They're all around me as I fidget in my fourth-period desk and stare at a "The Play's the Thing" banner hanging above the chalkboard: the kids who are the personifications of those boxes at the bottoms of forms that say Other.

Like in every other school—big, small, urban, country— we all get our brands the first day we walk in as freshmen. And are slammed into our chosen elective, herded off accordingly: the athletes toward the gym, the musicians toward the choir room, the doodlers—who illustrate their every math assignment—to pick out colored pencils from the art supply closet, the smarties toward debate or honors science. We move along for three years down prechosen tracks, like mechanical rats, until senior year, when we gather in our so-called specialty and undertake a giant collective "senior project"—last year the art kids all did a mural outside the cafeteria involving shiny garden vegetables. It caught a bit of online fire somehow, was retweeted fifteen hundred times. No joke.

At Verona High, drama is not a place for the wildly extroverted. It's not a place for anyone with any kind of burning theatrical desire. At Verona High, drama is for the shy, the foot shufflers, the shruggers who express no desire to stand out, the never-in-troubles, the rebelling-against-nothings. Good students who prefer the shadows. We're the colors in the crayon box that no one ever reaches for. Not the eye-catching colors: Atomic Tangerine and Shocking Pink. We're Burnt Sienna. Plain old Gray. We're never expected to make our mark at Verona High.

So there we are: for the most part, pretty good at most things but not likely to step up and say so. One row over, it also includes my best friend, Cass, who is the most incredible singer no one has ever heard. And just behind her, Dylan Michaels, who can, according to the owners of Ferguson's Music Store, play any instrument with strings but who has never performed for anyone. And me, who refuses to show anyone anything I've ever written. Because sometimes what makes a nobody is the fact that they don't have the burning desire to show off. Or maybe it's that they can't stand the idea of getting peeled back and critiqued on their most private thoughts. Or maybe it's that the spotlight doesn't fit everybody.

And here we sit. And nobody's breathing.

I squirm in my chair; the Indian summer heat's attacking me as relentlessly as the whack job in a Tarantino movie. My glasses keep slipping down my sweat-slicked nose. Large cursive letters left on the chalkboard promise, "After Lunch—Senior Project Announcement."

"It'll be bad," I hear behind me. "It's bound to be. My mom had her. *Horror* stories."

Cass swivels, tossing me a sympathetic stare. She knows when I need a reassuring wink or an eye roll. Like she's always known—ever since the days of afternoon naps and paste eating.

The classroom clock announces Mom's more than ten minutes late getting back from lunch when she finally stomps through the door.

"Really bad," another voice grumbles.

Mom's got that drill-sergeant look on her face. She flops a script on her desk, crosses her arms, and offers us one of her dramatic-effect pauses—the kind I've been the recipient of roughly twelve thousand times.

Mom—no, Ms. Drewery. It's Ms. Drewery when I'm in her classroom—came out of retirement to temporarily replace our former drama teacher, who was not a Ms. at all, but a Jenny. That's what we all called her, anyway. Jenny, who was so fresh out of college, she preferred to eat in the cafeteria with us instead of in the faculty lounge. Jenny, who wore jeans and glittery T-shirts and had short curly hair like Shirley Temple and swung her feet as she sat on top of the teacher's desk at the front of the room. Jenny, who got married last year and is currently on maternity leave. Jenny, who understood that we were not exactly Al Pacinos in training, and whose senior projects in the years leading up to our own senior stint involved asking all her students to memorize soliloquies or recite "Invictus" in unison.

But Jenny was not exactly a staff oddity. The rest of the instructors at Verona High usually rule with a pretty light touch. Small-town friendly atmosphere pervades the corridors—which are as antique as the rest of the buildings in town. Noisy pipes race through the halls beneath the ceiling, and Truman-era spackle fills the holes in most walls. It's a well-known fact that the hearts and initials carved into student desks belong to couples who've already celebrated silver wedding anniversaries.

So faculty makes up for the lack of ambience. Maybe we don't have some fancy modern glass-encrusted school, but we do have a meticulously mowed and fertilized football field, and a cafeteria serving comfort-food lunches prepared by the Verona women who grew up learning to cook in cast-iron skillets (and can make a stew of dirt and beef jerky taste like fine cuisine). And we have instructors who expect a little mischief now and again. Come on—what's a sophomore year without a good food fight? What's a senior year without a prank involving the school mascot, some Silly String, and the principal's car?

Faculty often refers to our "shenanigans" as minor earthquakes; they relieve the pressure, and as a result, litter rarely hits the hallways, library books are rarely overdue, and detention is a rarely needed punishment.

Now, though, Mom (Ms. Drewery—in room 235, it's always Ms. Drewery) is back after ten years. She's standing in front of the class in a midcalf wrinkled skirt and what look like old-fashioned nurse's shoes, her knee-high stockings rolled down to her ankles. She's staring at us over the top of the only pair of wire-framed glasses she's ever owned.

Not that anyone's staring at her outfit. They're staring instead at the words she's written on the chalkboard. And they're waiting. And nobody's breathing.

"They want to tear it down," Ms. Drewery proclaims as she begins to walk up and down the aisles studying every face.

The entire class turns into giant question marks.

"The Avery!" she shouts. "This is Advanced Drama, ladies and gentlemen. We must be aware when the city council threatens to destroy our town's theatrical history. They've never talked this way before. It was always just—a whisper, here and there. Discussions that were tabled at meetings. Now, though—it's serious."

I hear backsides sliding down into seats, heavy sighs.

"They're going to kill our last chance at revisiting the magic!"

I tense up, getting the decided urge to crawl into my backpack.

Nobody in this room has grown up listening to the story, not like I have. So when Mom uses the word "magic," it doesn't hit them in a literal way. And when someone insists the Avery's "dead," they only hear that the time for the Avery has come and gone. The days of going to a Sunday matinee dressed in gloves and a hat are completely over and done.

They do not believe the Avery Theater was once alive. They do not believe it had a heart that stopped beating in 1947. They do not believe it turned black right there on the square, under an aurora borealis light show, or that the sky promised the Avery would come back to life with the return of star-crossed lovers. That's the stuff of mostly forgotten urban legends. To them, the Avery is a building that became dilapidated over time. The end.

"You've never been inside that theater," Ms. Drewery goes on. To my left, Dylan ducks down behind his long bangs and starts squirming too. "But I have. I grew up there. And on that tragic night in 1947—the night the Avery—"

I hold my breath. *Don't say it, Mom. Don't say "died." Don't tell them the way you've told me. They'll all look at you like people used to look at Bertie.*

"—closed for good . . . ," she goes on, allowing me to

exhale. "You all know that story! Come on—it's part of our local folklore. Think about it. Imagine it. This happened in your town. That horrible story involves two people who were your own age. Emma probably sat in this very classroom at some point. She walked to one of those lockers in the hallway right outside this classroom door. Ate in the cafeteria just downstairs. After she and her boyfriend, Nick, died, there was never another production at the Avery. But there was always the hope that there would be. And now, instead of reinvigorating that beautiful theater, the city council wants to tear it down."

Maybe Ms. Drewery expects this to get everyone riled up, but nobody here is upset about the fact that the Avery's going to be torn down. Because Verona, Missouri, is not exactly filled with hipsters who would like to redo the old place, open it back up to play vintage cult classics. It's filled instead with people who work at the local hospital, check groceries at the Walmart Supercenter, or fix cars at the Ford dealership off the highway. They don't care that there used to be nearly thirty businesses on the square (counting the lawyers and dentists and accountants in second-story offices), and today only four doors remain with Open signs. No one—except me, Cass, and Dylan—ever semiregularly sets foot on the square. They all know the rest of Verona has moved on, farther south—kind of like the whole town is trying to get out of the city limits, move itself down the highway. No one has any interest in the

Avery—or the fact that the city council wants it demolished.

Me? I'm torn. I know what the Avery means. I know that Ms. Drewery has always dreamed of the Avery opening its doors again. I know she views it as the only real shot the town has of seeing business come back to the square. But at that moment, I'm more terrified of what she's got in store for us. If it's even a centimeter more involved than anything Jenny might've had us do, I'll pay for it. Why wouldn't I? She's my mother.

"We have the power to change their minds!" Ms. Drewery shouts. "We can save the Avery."

She picks up the script she carried into the room. *Oh, no, oh, no, oh, no.* The front is emblazoned with a giant bold "ANYTHING GOES."

I know exactly what she's thinking, even before her words come out. Because I remember what Mom said was on the marquee, every time she told me that bedtime story.

"We're going to do a production of *Anything Goes*!" she shouts. "The last community production to ever be shown at the Avery. Sell tickets. Raise money and interest. Convince the city council not to destroy such an important building."

Gasps dance through the room. Backsides slide up. Chests lean forward, over desks. The silence drips with fear.

"It's our senior project!" Ms. Drewery shouts. "Imagine! Saving the Avery—no other class will ever have such an impact on this town!"

But that's not what we do. We're Verona's drama class.

We memorize soliloquies. We walk by murals someone else painted that are admired on the internet. We step aside as the football team races down the hall, toward the field. That's us. Tramplees, not tramplers. *We don't make marks here, Mom. . . .*

"We have a great theatrical history here in Verona," Ms. Drewery insists. "Red carpets. First nights! It's time to bring it back. I'll post your cast assignments and supporting positions later today. We have a set to make, music to learn, costumes to design. We've got to get started."

A hand flies up. "Don't you have to get our senior projects approved by the principal?" It's a worthy attempt to buy time, to find an ally who might sympathize with us. To wage a battle against Ms. Drewery and her crazy plan. And of course only Kiki Ferguson would think of this angle. Kiki was once our playground tattletale, the kind of girl who would eye your skirt in the seventh grade and report you for having a hem an inch too short for the dress code, paragraph four of the student handbook. Examine the dioramas in fourth-grade science class so that she could report the inconsistencies to the instructor. The sort of girl who only got ahead by knocking the competition.

"He's already agreed. That's why I was late. As you know, the drama department has always been the first to reveal its senior project—usually in the fall semester, before the art department's winter exhibition."

Yes, Mom. Because we usually recite soliloquies.

"Which is perfect. We'll get this thing up and running—get some money flowing toward the Avery's renovations—right here at the start of the school year. When the city council's talking about it."

"But isn't it—too far gone?" another tries. "The Avery?"

"Too far gone!" Ms. Drewery thunders. "What a sad way to look at it. What you believe is what you see. And I'll tell you that I do not in any way see a curtain that has fallen on the last act. Just imagine, ladies and gentlemen. We're going to do the Avery's final production. We're going to finish its run right here in our own auditorium! And we're going to put enough money on the table that the city council will believe something different, too. See the Avery in a new way. Don't forget to come by the classroom after school. Your jobs will all be posted on a sheet I'll hang in the hallway. The rest of the student body will be able to see it on their way out, as well. Think of it as our first announcement! *Anything Goes*—to be performed by Advanced Drama! Yes!"

I can feel abject hatred being tossed my way. Nasty looks. Already, they've formed an anti-Drewery group. Even nobodies can join forces—form their own hierarchy.

And at this point, it appears as though I'm on the bottom rung.

three

Navigating the Verona High hallways has a decided upstream-salmon feel about it. Doesn't matter where I'm going—after all, Verona Consolidated High School was built for half its current population. And somehow, I'm always heading against the current.

Ever since Mom's fourth-period announcement, I swear the halls have also had a vicious feel. Between classes, elbow bumps have been hard enough to send me flying into all sorts of innocent bystanders. Swinging locker doors have jumped into my face, like pop-ups in a defensive-driving obstacle course. I've veered, I've lurched out of the way, I've kept my head down, trying to conceal my face.

By the time the three-o'clock bell rings and we're all back out in the hallway for the final time, I try to tell myself I'm imagining things. Of course I am. Because a handful of the Advanced Drama nobodies are suddenly at my side, and we're pressing forward, which is completely uncharacteristic of us. Forcing our way deeper into the school, hurrying to check out Mom's announcement sheet. We're in this thing together, fighting the stream of students filling the narrow corridors, all of them trying to get out of the building.

Cass takes hold of her seventies-era maxidress, pulling it up so that the bottom hem doesn't get tangled in her sandals. That thing's probably like a sweltering polyester cocoon, with the school's air conditioning barely even limping along. But that's not the reason for the heat that rolls from her shoulders.

Cass is worried. Like we all are.

When we finally make it back to room 235, the majority of the class has already congregated around Mom's door, pointing at the sheets of copy paper she's taped together to form one long white strip. Her letters are as large as a neon sign. Everyone's grumbling. Nobody's happy. There's a chorus of "Why'd she do that?" bubbling through the air.

I push my glasses up my sweaty nose, letting my eyes land on the bottom of Mom's cast list. My eyes move one step up the list with each beat of my heart, and my heart gets a little louder with each thump—like footsteps climbing stairs, getting increasingly closer. Until I make it all the way to the top of the list. And find it. My own name: Quin Drewery. And the horrific title: Director.

My head spins. I'm falling now, tumbling down every step I just climbed. Bouncing uncontrollably.

How could she do this to me? Director? No way. Everyone's already complaining. "Her mother made her the director?" "Of course she did." "Must be nice."

I haven't been imagining anything. I bet those hallway elbow jabs have been coming from Advanced Drama nobodies all day. All of them anticipating this very thing.

It looks like favoritism, Mom. Surely you knew that it would. Why'd you do this?

I glance into the classroom, but there's no sign of Mom—er, Ms. Drewery. It's like she's left her bomb and run, avoiding any of the flying shrapnel.

In front of me, Liz Garrison is shaking her head. Liz is the senior class mother in training. The type to buy you a cupcake from the dessert line in the cafeteria because you seem a little down, or offer you her cardigan when you sneeze. And beside me, Cass is saying, "No, no, no, no. I knew it. I *knew* she'd do this to me."

"What did you get?" I ask, afraid of her answer.

"Hope Harcourt."

"The lead?" I ask.

"The lead." Her hands fly to her head, her fingers weaving through her dirty-blond locks.

In front of me, Liz is still shaking her head. "Why would she pick me? For that? For *that*?" To emphasize her complete frustration, she throws her arms into the air at the same time she spins on her heel, ready to stomp off. But her hand brushes Cass's cheek.

Liz draws her hands back into her chest, and her eyes swell and her pink frosty mouth curls into a shocked O.

Cass flinches. Tugs at her hair to let it fall like a curtain across her face. But it's too late. The damage has been done. Liz and I both know it has.

Because when somebody has a giant port-wine stain down the entire right side of her face—like Cass does—the polite thing to do is to simply ignore it. Not draw attention to it by smacking it. Or letting your face show exactly how surprised—and maybe even a little grossed out—you are by the rough feel of the red cauliflower bumps.

We all know that.

And now Liz is more than embarrassed. Her face is getting even redder than Cass's birthmark. She doesn't know what to say, and her eyes have turned into pinballs because she can't even look Cass in the face.

I know I should do something to make up for Cass's hurt feelings. She always says she's used to it, this shocked—or awkward—response to her face. But you never get used to knowing that people are secretly thinking that whatever that thing is crawling down your forehead and cheek is every bit as bad as the gobs of greasy grimy gopher guts kids are always singing about on playgrounds.

Me—I'd forgotten about it a long time ago. And I don't mean "forget" in the way some people say, "Oh, I've forgotten the whole thing," when really, they're still carrying around a grudge. I mean it has slipped out of my sight, right out of my head. But isn't that what happens to unimportant things— like a graded math quiz from last semester or the receipt for a cash gas purchase? They fall out of your pocket or blow out the rolled-down window while you're driving. People are always losing their grip on insignificant things. The same way I always lose my grip on Cass's birthmark.

I don't see it. That is, until somebody—like Liz, who is still in the crowd hemming and hawing, her eyes darting around all over the place, rubbing the hand that had accidentally bumped into the birthmark—reminds me.

Dylan Michaels pushes me aside, just a few inches. He leans forward, squinting. But his squint turns into a full-on grimace when he finds his name. His hand flies to his forehead. *Musical Director.*

"W-w-w-whatt-t?" he stutters. As he always stutters. Even though speech therapists have been knocking on classroom doors, telling him it's time for his daily lessons, ever since elementary school. Whatever those therapists have tried to do for Dylan has never worked; the stutter has gotten harder, more permanent over time. Like a petrified tree turning to stone.

That's actually how everyone at Verona High treats him. Like a tree. People recognize his presence and walk around him, never expecting to have any real human interaction with him.

And now he's supposed to give musical direction? How?

I watch as Dylan's and Cass's eyes meet. The horrified looks on their faces show that they're picturing what their assignments actually mean. Cass is going to have to stand in the middle of a stage with a spotlight on her face. And Dylan is going to have to coach the cast through the songs, sending his voice across the auditorium every time we practice. And for the first time in their lives, they'll be forced to fully expose the one thing they feel the most insecure about.

Judging by the way everyone else is moaning, Cass and Dylan aren't alone. It's as though, after watching us for only a couple of weeks, Mom has zeroed in on the exact thing none of us would ever want to do and she's given it to us. Our new titles are all snakes jumping out of cans of peanut brittle. A gag gift that's not a gift—or funny—at all.

"Great," Cass says, looking straight at Dylan. "We're stuck with each other."

I know Cass means it as a way to commiserate with Dylan. The same way I know that she'll give a smile and wave to Liz the next time they bump into each other in the hallway.

Dylan hears it as disgust. She's hurt him. And like it's human nature to do, Dylan lashes out. He attacks back. A hurt for a hurt. He spits, "U-u-u-uuugly. Y-y-you're uuu-ggly!"

The word hits the air like a gunshot. It sounds mean. It is

mean. That was the intention. Only now, instantly, he's sorry. He shakes his head.

The rest of the students are making the same face that Liz wore a minute ago: round eyes, mouths curling into Os. No one knows how to smooth any of it over—least of all Dylan, who has already tucked his chin down toward his chest.

So we scatter.

four

Cass stays tight-lipped through the entire drive to the town square. I want to fix the way she feels. But I have no idea how. And maybe you can't, really, ever fix the damage done by a word. Especially *that* word. Especially when you're Cass. And "ugly" is exactly how you feel about yourself.

Shock and hurt swirl through her car (we take turns driving to school each day—kind of like the car version of the teeter-totters of our elementary school years), and my brain keeps searching for some kind of word Band-Aid for what's just happened. I can't think of a single thing, so I reach for the knob on the radio.

Cass parks outside of Duds Used Clothing, staring ahead blankly for a minute before finally killing the engine of her VW Bug. The old one, with the engine in the back.

We pull ourselves out, the only two people around on the town square.

As the name suggests, the Verona square is literally a square, which now, for the most part, feels like skeletal remains. The only open businesses left are Duds (where Cass works after school) on the west side, which stands next to a restaurant so ever-changing, the current business hasn't even invested in a real sign. It's only a piece of cardboard with a handwritten "Mexican Food" propped in the front window. Mom's store, Potions Perfumery, is on the south side; Ferguson's Music (where Dylan works after school) is on the east. The rest of the storefronts on all three sides are empty, dusty, filled with signs that beg for someone to rent them.

On the north stands the old Avery Theater—a building large enough to take up the entire side of the square. The saddest of all the dilapidated buildings, the Avery these days is an old woman whose family contends was once the town beauty. Any ornate gold detail has tarnished and blackened. Many of the windows are both broken and boarded up; several along the first floor are concealed by overgrown, wild shrubbery. The second story is marked by rotten windowsills, the glass of the windows all old enough to have turned purple. The roof is littered with thick, clumsy patches of black tar; old gargoyles are missing parts of their faces. Darkened bricks across the front of the building are tattooed with spray-painted warnings: "Keep Out!" "No Trespassing!!" "Stay AWAY!"

"I always dreamed about that place being open," Cass admits, pausing on the sidewalk to point at the old theater.

"Yeah," I say quietly. "I know." I hate the look Cass is wearing. The same look I figure most people wear when they're sentenced to jail time for something they didn't do.

"But this—I mean, I love the Avery. I love your mom. I love that she thinks I can—but I just—" She turns her pleading eyes toward me. "I don't think I can do this."

"But it won't be *you*," I try to reason. "Right? You'll be a character."

She doesn't answer.

The bottom of Cass's purple-and-blue floral print maxidress flutters around her ankles as she hurries into Duds.

Vanessa, the thirty-something owner who looks young enough to pass for our sister, glances up from the back of her point-and-shoot. She does her selling online—so much so, I always wind up wondering about the need for a storefront. Or an employee. But Cass would hang out here for free.

"Whoa. You guys get in a wreck on your way over here?" she asks. "What's with the faces?"

"Mom's decided we're doing a production of *Anything Goes*. In order to raise money for the Avery," I tell her.

"That's kind of fantastic, though, isn't it? I thought you two were always interested in that place. Aren't you the one," she goes on, looking right at me, "who told Cass about what happened inside? To those two kids? And didn't you get all teary-eyed about it? Get so worked up about it that you used the word 'died'? The old place 'died,' you said. How sad it all was. Now your mom's trying to save the place and you still look sad. Isn't saving the Avery a good thing?"

"Cass got the lead," I say. "Hope Harcourt."

Vanessa swivels in time to watch Cass rake her fingers through her dirty-blond hair in a way that makes it tumble over the birthmark.

"Oh," Vanessa grumbles. She's still staring. Still trying to think of something to say.

But my *you'll be another person on the stage* line of reasoning didn't exactly make Cass feel any better, and I'm a little afraid if Vanessa says anything at this point, Cass might burst into tears. So I point toward a rack in the back—the one with the records—and say, "How can you stand to work in here without a soundtrack keeping you company?"

While Duds is primarily a vintage-clothing store—the place is crammed with round mirror-topped dress racks labeled by the decade—plenty of pop culture gems fill the side shelves, too: Enid Collins box bags and disco ball–shaped 8-track players and lava lamps and flatware with Bakelite handles. And records, in the back corner. A sign above a nearby turntable invites shoppers to pick out any of the albums up for sale and set them spinning.

"I just had on some classic Queen, for your information," Vanessa says, obviously grateful for a chance to change the subject. "Feel free to continue on with the metal fest. I'm obviously in the mood today." She stands, pointing toward the Van Halen '81 Worldwide Tour concert T-shirt she's paired with an acid-washed jean skirt.

Together, as usual, Vanessa and Cass make me feel horribly underdressed. Or maybe the right term's "understyled." While Vanessa and Cass both have the vintage thing going for them, I'm in my usual khaki shorts and plain, solid-colored T-shirt. I haven't done anything to my shoulder-length brown hair other than brush it—a widow's peak makes it impossible to do something strategic with the front of it. The only things about my daily appearance that really show much pizazz are my glasses. Cass bought them from Duds for my last birthday: forest-green cat's eyes with blue rhinestones in the pointy corners. I had prescription lenses put in.

But today I couldn't care less about feeling a little less than special in the outfit department. Not with Cass's mouth still turned down. Since my own mom's the one who's given her this role, I feel like I'm the one responsible for making her upset. I feel like it's my job to fix it.

"You got it," I tell Vanessa. Because vintage metal has nothing to do with the theater. So maybe if I can find another record in this stack, one that gets us all dancing around the store in a goofy way, it will soothe something inside Cass.

I've just started to flip through the vinyl when the front door flops open. And in walks Liz. The same Liz from Advanced Drama.

"Hey, Cass," she says in a perky voice. *What is she doing here?*

Cass looks every bit as confused as I feel—until Liz says, "I thought I should probably go ahead and get started."

"On what?" Cass asks.

"The costumes," Liz says.

"*You're* in charge of costumes?" Cass asks sadly.

I look at Vanessa, who shakes her head. Liz fidgets, tugging at her blue sundress. That tug is surely meant to remind Cass that she does, in fact, show up in a dress every single day. That maybe there really are good reasons why she got the costume gig. In response, Cass crosses her arms over her chest, emphasizing the fact that she's got a bright-yellow shirt tied at the waist over her blue-and-purple maxidress. She's reminding Liz that there are all sorts of reasons why she wears such funky outfits—sure, she wants to take attention away from her birthmark. But she also has a great love of all things vintage. The bottom line is that Cass knows clothes. Cass would have been far more comfortable handling the costumes than being Hope Harcourt. Cass wants Liz's gig. Resents Liz for the gig—more, even, than she feels bad about the hallway scene. It's more than obvious to both me and Vanessa—but Liz remains clueless.

"Do you have anything from that era? It's the thirties, right?" Liz asks, beginning to flip through a rack of blouses near the checkout counter.

"It'll depend on everyone's sizes," Cass mutters, tugging on her lip as she turns toward another rack—this one filled with older dresses and skirts. "We can probably get by going with some basic shapes, some silhouettes that are reminiscent of the time but are actually newer garments."

There it is—the positive sign that Liz has been after. She exhales loudly, obviously interpreting Cass's words as a *That's okay, Liz. All forgiven.* She blurts, "Congrats on the lead."

Cass pauses, her hand hovering over a hanger, ignoring Liz's remark.

"What a crazy coincidence!" Liz shouts. And giggles.

Cass and I both glance up as Liz points toward the display of records. The *Anything Goes* cast recording.

"That's Cass's album," I say. "Most of the musical theater albums in here are hers. For sale on consignment."

"That's the 1962 off-Broadway cast recording, with Eileen Rodgers and Hal Linden," Cass explains, her words clipped. Liz is still treading on fragile ground. "I prefer the 2011 Sutton Foster version."

"Then you know the musical already! Good for you!"

Cass and I both flinch against Liz's slightly condescending tone.

Liz leans forward, now judging herself to be one of Cass's close friends—and entitled to give her advice. "You know, if you're worried about it, you could use Dermablend. My sister uses it to cover up a tattoo."

A smack. This is a smack. Another one. How could Liz be so dense? I'm about to speak up when Cass sucks in her breath and tightens her fist. "I've tried it," she mutters.

"It—doesn't work?"

"It bleeds through after a while. And the skin's still bumpy. So even with a perfect color cover-up—"

"Oh. I just thought. You know. From the audience, they wouldn't see—"

"Everyone knows it's there, anyway," Cass says, trying to shrug off another attack.

"Doesn't your dad work at the hospital?"

Cass frowns. "He's an anesthesiologist," she says quietly, afraid of where this is headed.

"Did he—is it—inoperable?" Liz whispers.

Vanessa swivels. My eyes widen behind my glasses. Liz has gone way too far. But Cass continues, almost as if she's talking to herself. "Dad said I wasn't the world's best candidate for removal treatments. And it requires several visits. And the treatments, while maybe not painful in the sense of having your right foot smashed by a Hummer, aren't exactly a pleasurable day on the massage table, either. And there's always a chance that the treatments could actually make the birthmark darker. And, after all that, even if it worked, the birthmark could always come back.

"Besides," Cass adds sarcastically, "a birthmark is harmless. It isn't cancer, and it isn't a bullet hole, and it isn't a giant pile of gangrene that makes bits of rotting flesh fall from my skull into my Cheerios every morning."

"Oh, I didn't—"

"Why don't you read the script before you look for costumes?" Cass suggests. This is a scolding. Even Liz knows that.

Liz nods slowly. She heads reluctantly for the door, clearly not wanting to leave on this note.

We all watch her slip back outside. At the same time, on the opposite side of the front window, the city bus rolls to a stop. Dylan gets off, tugging his bike down the bus steps, and heads straight toward Ferguson's Music.

"Hey. There's—" I start.

"Yeah. And we get to work together for the rest of the play. Yay."

"Why don't I go over there and talk to him? Get some ideas rolling for first practice. The director and the musical director will have to work closely—"

"No," Cass moans. "That's not why you're going over

there. I can read your mind. And I've had more than enough for today. Seriously. Let the whole thing drop. Okay?"

"No way," I say. "Someone needs to clear the air before the first rehearsal. And this is my mess, too. I've got to direct you guys, right?"

"Quin! Don't!"

But I'm already out the door.

five

I race to the opposite side of the square and throw open the door of Ferguson's Music, where I find Dylan digging through a plastic bin propped on the front counter. I take a few steps inside, but he's too intent on his search to glance up.

"What are you doing?" a voice thunders at the same point the door flies open again.

It's Kiki Ferguson, with her wild orange hair and a vicious scowl carved into her face. But then again, in addition to her incredibly attractive tattling addiction, Kiki's always had a decidedly nasty streak. She probably frowns in her sleep. Growls with disgust at pictures of puppies.

It could only happen in small towns or soap operas (where the same fifteen characters keep bumping into one another over and over), but yes, this is the same Kiki from Advanced

Drama. And her family is the Ferguson in Ferguson's Music. And here she is. Staring at me and Dylan.

It's not just a nasty look that Kiki has on her face—it's protective, too. Like the old guy in the neighborhood who shouts at kids to get off his lawn. Which is beyond odd. Kiki has, since middle school or so, talked about Ferguson's Music like it's a burden. She's refused to work there, preferring instead to flip burgers at the Sonic off the highway in the summer. She wants to take over the family business like most sixteen-year-old boys want to take over their father's appliance stores.

What's she even doing here? I wonder. Usually, Kiki spends as little time as possible on the square. Stops by every few months when her dad (still hopeful that she'll eventually take an interest in the store, passed down for the last three generations) ropes her into doing inventory.

I've always figured Kiki really did inherit the Ferguson music gene—that the lessons her dad forced on her (everything from guitar to voice to tuba) really did sink in. But like anyone else in Advanced Drama, she's never been the sort to form garage bands or post YouTube cover videos.

"T-t-t-ttttt—" Dylan attempts. "T-tt-t-tttttt-t—" as his sweaty hands leave silver streaks all over the glass counter. "T-ttttt—*ool,*" Dylan finally manages, at the same moment that Kiki reaches the counter.

"You know, Dylan," Kiki grumbles, "if I wanted to cool off in a sprinkler, I would run through one." She scowls, acting as if she's wiping his spit from the side of her nose. In reality, she's sweating buckets from the unnatural heat that's settled across Verona.

He fishes an order form from his shorts and slides it across the counter toward Kiki, who keeps pawing at her wilted face. She smears her sloppy, gunky makeup until her cheeks look like pools of half-melted ice cream. He points at the form. "V-v-v-voi-c-ce t-t-t-*tool*." He says the last word with such force, the overly long front of his hair bounces against his forehead. He shakes his head once to knock the sharp ends of his thick brown bangs from his eyes.

As he moves, a necklace falls out from the top of his T-shirt. It's a skeleton key on a cord. He grabs it, tosses it back inside his shirt.

But not before I notice.

"Why are you going through the orders yourself?" Kiki snaps. "Why aren't you waiting for Dad? He's in the back. He'll be out any minute. Besides, you fix instruments. You're not supposed to work the cash register."

"C-c-can y-you j-jjjustt . . ."

"C-c-c," Kiki mimics.

Dylan's shoulders sink. He is a bull's-eye, a clay pigeon, a punching bag. The easiest target in the entirety of Verona's public schools. Always has been. Anytime someone's upset, they feel free to stop ignoring Dylan long enough to take their aggravations out on him.

"How are you going to manage that gig? Musical director. Please."

"You don't have any other customers—nobody's around—so why don't you just give him what he wants?" I ask.

When Dylan sees me, he recoils like a wild animal who isn't quite sure, when you come out the back door to find him standing in your yard, if you're going to offer him a bowl of water or shoot him with a BB gun.

Kiki turns a set of narrow eyes my way. "Giving orders already? Settling into that director role? Must be really nice."

I shrug. I have no problem putting myself in the way of Kiki's personality—which is a little like jumping in front of a honking Mac truck. I've had my fill of snippiness and nastiness. Cass is right—we've all had more than enough for one day.

"He's obviously paid for it, though," I argue.

"And I guess you know all about running a music store. *I've* been around this place my whole life. Maybe not by choice—but still. He's going to have to come to me to rent any equipment he needs. Why not ask me to be musical director? Why put me onstage?"

There it is, the reason for this particular attack: she's upset about Dylan getting the gig she'd apparently wanted. Being musical director must look better to her than being assigned a role. Her frustration is spewing out everywhere, like water from a busted hose.

Kiki glances into the bin, shakes her head. "The whole thing is dumb," she mutters. "The Avery. Please. A fund-raiser for a corpse." And stomps off, disappearing into the back.

"Th-thanks," Dylan breathes, and stares at the bin.

"She doesn't like her assignment," I say. "She probably only came to the square today to punish you for getting her gig. You're always here. You love this place. Which is surely why Mom gave you the musical director job."

He nods limply, refusing to lift his eyes from the bin.

"If the world were fair, you'd be in line to inherit Ferguson's Music." I try to chuckle.

Still, he stares into the bin. Like he doesn't want to look me in the eye.

"You didn't mean it," I say.

When he glances up, a blank look on his face, I go on. "In the hallway. At school. You didn't mean it. That insult to Cass."

He exhales with relief. Nods. "Sh-she ww-aas b-being rr-otten," he says. "Wh-whatt sh-she sssaidd w-was ug-gly."

"About you guys being stuck together?"

He nods, sticking his hand back in the bin of special orders.

"She didn't mean it in a bad way, either, you know. Just that you guys are in the same boat. We all are."

"Tt-tell h-her I'mmm s-sor-r-ry."

"I will." I nod to his hand. "What is that thing?"

Dylan pulls out a horrific-looking tool with needles poking out the front. It almost looks like a tattoo gun.

"Vv-v-voice tttt-ool. F-for the pppiano."

He eyes that tool in a way that makes me wonder how many times Dylan's dreamed of sitting on some paper-lined examination table, saying, "Ahhh," and letting a doctor hit him a few times with his own voicing tool. *Voilà!* Instant fix. No more bearing the brunt of snickers. No more being an easy target—like the one that Kiki's turned him into.

But we're classmates. Not friends. We exchange polite hallway smiles. If one of us stepped on the other's toes in the lunch line, we would apologize and fall into awkward silence. We are not the sort who unload on each other—share a bunch of painfully private thoughts. The voicing tool is making us both uncomfortable. Instead of stepping on a toe, one of us has caught the other coming out of the gym shower completely nude.

I need to get this back to our comfort zone: acquaintance-level chitchat. So I smile and ask, "Are you working on a piano in the store?"

He shakes his head.

"Where, then? Is that what the key around your neck is for?" I bite my lip. That was dumb. Just as we were getting comfortable again, there I had to go, prying in a way that polite nonfriends never do.

He puts a finger to his lips as he starts to pull away, heading toward the back of the store. "A m-mannn nn-needs hh-is s-secrett-ts."

six

Cass is on the sidewalk outside Duds when I leave Ferguson's. She's mucking around with one of those easel signs—the kind with a marker board on both sides. This one advertises a fall sale on sweaters that seems a bit cart-before-the-horse, actually, in the midst of the Indian summer heat. The entirety of Verona feels every bit as hot as the steering wheel of a car after three solid hours of sitting out in an August parking lot.

But it's not the sign she's interested in. She's staring at the music store, waiting. For me.

"He didn't mean you," I insist as soon as she's within earshot. "What he said—'ugly.' He meant what you *said* was ugly—he took it wrong."

She keeps staring, unconvinced. Or maybe she's waiting

for a better explanation.

"He's afraid of his job, too, you know. Musical director. That's terrifying for him."

Still. She stares. Weighing this answer, trying to decide if she believes me.

"Okay, you got me. I spent the whole time I was gone beating him to a pulp. That store has his blood splattered all over the tile."

She tosses her head back and laughs. "That's more like it. I could go with that. Finally, a perfectly triumphant end to the world's crummiest day."

I grab her around the neck and squeeze. Her laughter always makes me want to scoop her into a giant best-friend hug. This afternoon, though, her laughter is especially soothing to us both. It's lavender scented. It's soft and tastes good. Finally. Laughter.

After our usual round of "See you in the a.m.," I practically skip to Potions.

Mom's not home yet, so I unlock the front door, gratefully tossing my backpack under the cash register. I could go for some time alone, some breathing space before she gets here. Some time to quit thinking about school completely. Because the minute she shows up, it'll be the Avery and *Anything Goes* and my being a director of the whole ridiculous shebang that brings a sick, heavy feeling to my gut.

But for now, there's just the store—just my home. And

quiet. And the lingering smell of Mom's latest batch of perfume—in which she's somehow captured the smell of overcoats
and chocolate and snow and a swirl of different brands of soap
and leather and hair spray and even popcorn. An interesting
assortment completely unlike the floral scents that usually
permeate the entire shop.

I flick on a few lights and head into the back room, where
I find Mom's already started to package this new scent. A
whole tray is nearly filled with squat little bottles ready for
sale. I pick one up, look at the sticker on the bottom. Mom's
calling this batch Sunday Matinee.

I smile. The Avery's taken front row in her mind—surely
because of the city council thing. She hadn't said anything
to me about it—that announcement in class was the first I'd
heard of the idea to tear down the Avery. But those kinds of
things don't pop up out of nowhere. Mom's known this deci-
sion's been coming for a while.

I feel a little bit blindsided, actually. And every bit as
unsure of being able to get through it as Cass is.

Maybe, I think, a little work is what I need. Distrac-
tion. Sometimes, a simple job that takes you out of your head
can feel every bit as good and comforting as a holey favorite
T-shirt . . . or laughter from a best friend.

I could make a nice new front-window display, I figure.
That's exactly the kind of task that will steer my thoughts
down a new direction. Let me pretend, for a little while,

that the pit in my stomach doesn't actually exist. Our supply closet offers up a few artificial silk flowers—mums, in fiery orange shades. I carry them and the tray of bottles to the front window. I stare across the street at the theater that I've never actually been inside of but has somehow also been such a central part of my life.

Maybe it's because Dahlia adopted me when I was still an infant, but my ancestry never seemed like something I could plot out on one of those single-family trees. It's always seemed like a giant connect-the-dots picture. I mean, here I am, working in the same front window where Dahlia's own mom was changing out a hat display the night two kids my age died in the Avery. I'm staring out at the same square where Bertie, my real biological great-grandmother, stood mumbling her usual gibberish about what the skies were saying. I'm standing in the same place where Mom grew up. The store she took over, reinvented, and saved when her own mother died—like she saves everything. Including me, a baby found in the backseat of a totaled car, no living relatives.

It's so weird, the way everything is connected: me, Mom, Bertie, Emma and Nick (two kids who never had a chance to make it to nineteen), the Avery. All of us dots. And if I could ever figure out the order I should connect us all in, I know it'd make some kind of picture. Up until now, though, the picture I've always drawn in my mind winds up looking like a giant confused scribble.

"I promised I'd save Emma." That sentence floats through my head. Sometimes when Mom told me the bedtime story about the night the Avery died, instead of the usual bright promise for "magic" to return, for the Avery to come back from the dead, she would whisper, "I promised I'd save her." As though it was a detail so painful, she could only repeat it on the nights when she was feeling especially brave. This, too, this need to save everything—it seems like another dot in the picture. Not that I'm sure where it fits in, either.

I only know that when Mom inherited the store, nobody was wearing hats anymore. No more new pillboxes or cloches to dress up old suits. Oh, come on. Who was even wearing suits? Now, the perfumery she's turned the old hat store into is barely getting any foot traffic. Pile on the fact that Mom's temporarily back in the classroom (leaving the store open only on afternoons and weekends), and there's really not much sense in me spending time on a front-window display. But it feels good to clear my head. So much so, I lose track of the time.

I don't look up from my display until Dylan leaves Ferguson's a couple of hours later. His movement on the opposite side of the window finally grabs my attention. *A man needs his secrets.* Isn't that what he said? What kind of secrets does Dylan have? I press my face against the front window, curious to see where he'll go. He throws his leg over his bike and pedals away.

I flip the Closed sign, burst out of the store, and race off the front sidewalk. But I get less than a foot into the square when I stop. Dylan's steered down the alley behind the Avery and is already out of sight. And I'm not sure which direction he headed in once he hit that alley. I'll never catch up.

I laugh at myself. Nosy busybody. What business is it of mine where he's going? What do I think I am, the director of everybody's life?

Bleah. Director. It hits me again.

I'm about to turn back around, head into the shop, when Cass bursts outside—finished with her shift at Duds.

"Hey, Ca—" I start to call out to her, but stop when I hear another sound floating through the air and across the square.

Musical notes. Muffled. Tinny. Off-key.

Like an old piano.

seven

I'm mesmerized. Rooted to my spot in front of Potions. Those notes seem to be spilling directly from the ancient and long-empty Avery. No one's been inside for years—longer than I've been alive. I've never seen the building when it wasn't boarded up and vacant. And now, out of nowhere, someone is in the old theater, playing music, la-di-da, no big deal?

Maybe it's some kind of weird coincidence—maybe the Avery's been on my mind all afternoon, and maybe I just want music to be coming from the old theater.

Only, as I stand there trying to come to grips with it all, I turn and see Cass stopping beside her driver's-side door. She shades her eyes with her hand and stares right at the old theater. She's heard the music, too. The piano sounds out of tune and kind of metallic—like an old-fashioned harpsichord.

She walks apprehensively toward the Avery. As though in a trance, she moves down the long front walk that stretches from the street all the way to the entrance. Dead brown weeds poking from the cracks in the cement are tall enough to completely swallow her feet. Above, the cloth awning that once stretched over the entirety of the walk is so tattered, it really isn't anything other than a metal frame decorated with rotten fragments of cloth. Cass can look up and see the whole marquee, dark for nearly seventy years. The yellow neon letters, which spell "Avery Theater," are broken, marked with a couple of bird's nests.

Like a child edging into "off-limits" territory, Cass tiptoes to the front door, held closed by a rusty chain and padlock. She presses her ear against the dirty wooden door. Then cups her hands around her face, trying to peer through one of the last remaining windows that haven't been covered with plywood. Trying to see where the music's coming from.

Cass sits down on the front step, hugs her knees, and rocks gently to the rhythm of the repeating chord. I cup my mouth to shout, "Hey—what are you doing? You hear that, right? What is that?" But I stop as I get the feeling that if I were to call to her, she'd yelp and jump like I'd scared her out of a daydream.

She tilts her head and begins to sing—no distinct words, just a melody she improvises to blend with the notes bleeding through the walls of the theater.

The piano begins to respond, playing more complicated runs to go along with Cass's pretty tune.

There's something kind of hypnotic about the way the off-kilter chord mixes with Cass's voice. It becomes junk food for my ears. I want another taste, but know at the same time that another taste is only going to make me want still more.

The late-afternoon sun is brutal. I'm sweating, and my fair skin has begun to let out those *getting scorched here* warning signals.

That is, until a cloud slides between me and the sun, dragging a silky-cool breeze across my skin.

I turn my head skyward, ready to unleash an "Ahhh" or "Thank you."

My smile vanishes, though, when I find myself staring not at a white cloud's underbelly, but at a midnight darkness that has inexplicably appeared over the square. Night has fallen. Stars glitter. The moon hovers.

"What—" I mumble as I shudder against a sudden chill. Confusion and fear swirl; a row of exclamation points fills my head. *What is this?*

A siren cries in the distance.

I tremble, confused and startled, as a tiny yellow light flashes maybe a foot from my face. A firefly, blinking adamantly. It shouldn't be here—no more than a night sky should appear in the middle of the day. Firefly season starts early in

Missouri summers, and disappears long before the first freeze. But it's September, and the fireflies should all be gone.

Fighting to make sense of it all, I latch onto the fact that it's been unusually hot—hotter, even, than most Indian summers. The fireflies have hung on because of the lingering summer heat, I tell myself.

But the night—where has that come from?

It can't be night. How stupid. Night doesn't fall in late afternoon, all at once, out of nowhere. *Come on, Quin, where's your head?*

Maybe it's a low-flying plane hovering over the square. Or an eclipse. Something decidedly boring and realistic that will explain it all.

Only, when I look up again, there is no simple answer. Just a dark sky with stars. A moon. Streetlights pop to life in front of the theater.

When a firefly flitters in front of my face again, I swoop my hand out in a sorry attempt at catching it. I want to touch it, this thing that shouldn't be here, no more than that night sky should be. If I catch it, if I conquer it, then maybe whatever has overtaken the entire Verona sky won't be quite so frightening, either.

But I'm too slow—the firefly zips away, landing on the small, grassy lawn in front of the Avery. Or the scraggly brown patch that passes for a lawn, anyway. And then it rises— higher, higher, toward the empty marquee and the broken neon Avery Theater sign. It hovers there, blinking insistently. If I allow my eyes to wander even for a slice of a second, the firefly edges into my line of sight, then flitters back toward the front of the theater.

Goose bumps spill down my arms. What's happening? Is the firefly pointing? Telling me where to look?

A sudden pop from the front of the Avery sends a shower of orange sparks exploding across the night sky.

The old dilapidated neon Avery Theater sign flicks to life, glowing yellow. The marquee buzzes, emitting a high-pitched electric hum. The marquee promises, "TONIGHT! EMMA HASTINGS AS HOPE HARCOURT IN ANYTHING GOES!"

The streetlights continue to shine on the Avery as brightly as spotlights. It can't be! But it is—the building has begun to mend like a wound healing on fast forward. Boards vanish from windows. Graffiti fade. Cracks running like jagged lightning bolts through the mortar between bricks disappear. Animated expressions replace the weather-worn blank faces of gargoyles. The awning repairs itself, covering a suddenly smooth, paved front walk. Wild, overgrown arms of untrimmed bushes shrink, making shrubs appear well manicured. Grass begins to grow lush and green. Vines creeping along the edges of the building swell with buds threatening to burst open.

The Avery—that slobbering old woman everyone swears

once had an endless string of suitors—is young again. She's risen from the dead.

I want to scream, but my throat's too tight for any sound to escape.

The harmony of the piano and Cass's voice grows louder.

Other than the theater, the square remains unchanged: the modern neon "Ferguson's" light continues to glow over the music store's door, and a Corona sign burns in the window of the Mexican restaurant. Vanessa moves about on the opposite side of the Duds plate glass. Behind me, Potions is just as I left it, my own display gracing the front window.

Cass's voice continues to mingle with the piano. I stare at her sitting on the front step, still swaying to her music. Are her eyes closed? How can she have missed this transformation? Am I the only one who sees it?

Footsteps click down the street. *Someone sees.*

A woman races toward me, wearing a red-and-white striped seersucker dress that rustles about her knees.

"You see it, too," I whisper when she gets close enough to hear me. "The night sky. The Avery. You see it."

She faces me, and I get the odd sensation I'm looking into a mirror. She has my brown hair, my widow's peak, and a crook in her nose nearly identical to the one I like to say holds my glasses in place. I know this woman. But this cannot be real.

"Of course I see it," she says, smiling. "I was the one

who said it would happen. And now everyone will know I was right." She crosses her arms, hugging a red journal to her chest. "Alberta" has been scrawled across the front in cursive. My trembling intensifies. Bertie is short for Alberta.

"Where'd you get that book?"

"It's mine," she says as if I should already know.

"How—"

"Dahlia's been keeping it safe," she explains, holding the journal under my nose. "She promised she would. Look how clean and perfect it is. What a good job she's done."

"Dahlia—that's—my mom."

Bertie uncrosses her arms to point behind my shoulder, where yellowish-green flames leap from the horizon, climbing into the dark sky. "Look, Quin. It's come back. Just like I said it would." Satisfaction washes across her face as she whispers, "It's them."

How can she know my name? "Who's 'them'?" It's all I can manage.

"Don't pretend you don't hear them." Bertie points at the front of the theater. "Their duet has unlocked the story. They've brought the sky back. They've brought the past back. It's picking up where it once ended far too soon. The next scene is unfolding."

Her eyes flash brightly as she opens her arms. Her journal, which she now clutches by a corner, flops open; the pages flip back and forth in the breeze, as though some invisible hand is searching for the right passage.

"Picking up?" I repeat as I glance up at the stars.

"This isn't just any night sky," Bertie tells me. "It's the night sky of June 27, 1947."

The night sky of my bedtime stories.

"You'll see, don't worry. This is really happening," Bertie continues, her voice calm. "Two pure hearts meant to be together. There will be a new ending. Star-crossed lovers uncrossed."

"What does that even mean? What pure hearts?"

"Cass and Dylan, of course. You hear their music. Her voice, his chords."

"Dylan? He's meant to be with Cass? What are you talking about?"

"And you," Bertie whispers. "You're part of it, too. You had to be here. For all this to happen."

"Me? What do I have to do with it?"

Bertie cocks her head to the side. "You believe in it, don't you?"

"Believe in what?"

"The magic of the theater, of course."

The piano music ends abruptly. Just as quickly, Cass stops improvising.

A slit appears in the center of the awning; the fabric turns brown and withers. The awning becomes nothing more than a tarnished metal frame with only tattered bits of material clinging on for dear life. Vines and grass and bushes crackle as they dry up and turn brown.

The late-night sky slips away, exposing billowy white clouds and a powder-blue sky.

The Avery shrivels. Graffiti rewrite themselves across the bricks. Boards slap loudly against the windows. Gutters rust. The front walk cracks and buckles. Features are scrubbed from the faces of the gargoyles along the top of the building. The screaming siren grows faint, as though it's changed direction—as though it's driving away from the Avery rather than coming closer. The angry heat of the Indian summer returns.

"What—what—?" I sputter. But the street beside me is empty. Bertie's gone.

Cass's sandals click as she races down the Avery's front walk.

The tiny jingle of a small chain and the *whoosh* of wheels draw my eyes toward the side of the building. I watch as Dylan emerges from the alley, hops on his bike, and begins to pedal frantically. In his hurry to get away, though, his handlebars wobble, and his front tire zigzags along the cracked pavement. Before I can shout a warning, Cass walks straight into Dylan's path.

Cass lets out a yelp as Dylan punches his brakes, trying to stop.

He teeters toward the ground, throwing his leg out to the side to catch himself. "H-h-h-h-hey-ey-ey-ey!" he shouts, because she's nearly knocked him to the ground, where the rough pavement of the square could have completely chewed up his bare arms and knees.

Cass only veers around him without a word. Heads straight for her car. Dylan whips off in the opposite direction.

And I'm left standing alone.

I shake my head. Can three nobodies from Verona High Advanced Drama unlock anything?

No way.

. . . Or could we?

eight

I turn away from the Avery, my head a blender. I'm short of breath, and my legs are as sturdy as water.

None of what I've witnessed feels real—and somehow also more real than anything I've ever lived through. The colors were brighter. The music was clearer. *What just happened?*

Mom's car is now parked outside of Potions. She's been home long enough that all the lights are on in our apartment. How did I not hear her car? See her pause on the sidewalk to open the door? I stumble inside. Up the stairs.

"I know what you're going to say," she announces as I drag myself into the kitchen, my mouth dangling half open.

"You—you saw?"

"Oh, I saw. I know exactly what went on."

"What—what is—"

"Pure anger. That's what. I know kids. Taught enough years to know exactly what the reaction was going to be. That *Jenny* teacher of yours was letting you take the easy way out. Recite soliloquies for your senior project, my foot," she says, attacking a carrot with a knife. "People will always rise to the occasion. Expect nothing, get nothing."

"What're you talking about?"

"Cass! Of course! Don't play innocent, Quin. I know she's upset. I saw the way she reacted in class when I made the announcement about the musical. That look on her face! But I was around during all those sleepovers you kids've been having since you were—what? Seven? All those nights with her right here in this apartment, singing to whatever music you two happened to be into at the time. There's no way I'd give her the costumes job. And don't tell me that's not what she wants. I know her well enough to know that, too. Costumes." She shakes her head in disgust.

"But—the Avery—"

"Yes! The Avery is depending on us. It's about to see the wrecking ball. We're its last hope. We've got to do something. It's up to us."

She hadn't seen it. Not the night sky, or the lights blazing on the marquee. She hadn't seen her old friend, either. *Mom, Bertie was just out there, on the street. I didn't recognize her at first. But she wasn't a dream. She couldn't have been. She was so clear, and it was like looking into a mirror. She was just there, and she was talking about you.*

But do I tell her? She's been filling me with the details of a tale of magic for years. Part of me wants to scream at her that it's here, it's happened. But the other part is shouting out warnings. Since when does magic hide? If the magic wanted Mom to see it, wouldn't it have shown its face to her? I mean, it seemed like what was happening on the square lasted a few seconds. A single moment. But judging by the smells of long-simmering pots, I'd say Mom's been here at least thirty minutes. Magic had plenty of time to get Mom's attention.

But it didn't. It got mine.

Is that what I'm really thinking? That it was the magic Bertie promised all those years ago? Of course not. That's nuts.

Only, it's not. And as much as I could try to play it cool about the whole thing, the truth is, my heart believes it. All of it. Believed from the moment the first spark flew from the front of the Avery. It's just taking my brain a while to catch up. But then again, brains are always slow, lagging behind the lightning speed of the heart. The thought finally forms, clearly in my head: *I believe.*

"And you're upset, too," Mom adds.

"I'm upset—"

"Because I made you director."

"Daughter of the teacher is named director? You have to

know how that looks. Why aren't *you* the director? Isn't the teacher usually—"

"I'm the producer. I have to be. To get ads lined up—get some backing. Spread the word. Get the community riled up enough to buy tickets. This is going to require more than thirty sets of parents showing up, you know."

"But there has to be someone better. I have no idea—"

"You're a writer—it's in you. You know about characters."

I stare at her, my eyes feeling about as big as those velvet paintings of kids that Vanessa's got for sale in Duds.

"Oh, come on, Quin. You write. I wish you'd own up to it. You know how to develop characters. So explain their roles to the kids playing them. Tell them what their motivation is. You also understand the kids I've assigned a part to. Every bit as much as you understand the kids we're doing this for."

"The kids we're doing this for?" I repeat slowly.

She sighs with complete exasperation. Like there's no way I can be this dense. "Emma. Nick."

I shake my head. "What do they have to do with anything? That's just some story. A sad one. But a story. And one that happened decades ago." I'm challenging her. Goading her. I need something, after what I just saw. And I'm not sure what. Some kind of affirmation. Some new tidbit she's never shared before.

"Just—" Mom drops her knife. "You, of all people, should know there's no such thing as just a story. 'Just a story,' she says!" She shakes her head at me. "Come here."

I trail her through the apartment, toward my room, where the books have completely taken over. Mom's right—I'm a full-on story addict. She's always been my enabler, picking up paperbacks every single time she goes to the grocery store. And what kind of decent holiday season doesn't involve a good ten or so fat new novels?

I've never had the ability to throw a book away, either, once I've read it. So the ones I've already gobbled up have actually become my furniture; stacked hardbacks have become my nightstand, supporting an alarm clock and small boudoir lamp. Another tower of already-read books has become shelving for my winter sweaters.

Mom attacks my closet, pulling out old hatboxes. She's saved them, too—the old boxes from her mother's storeroom. She's stuck white labels to their sides, branding them with her perfect handwriting, and turned them into storage units. In her closet, the labels read "Taxes" or "Quin's Photos" or "Christmas." In mine, the labels read "Fifth Grade" or "Summer Camp" or "Cass and Me." The labels also read "Quin Stories," "Quin Stories 2," and "Quin Stories 3." Ten of them in all. Everything I've ever scribbled: little sketches, fragments of poetry, full-on short stories. I write them, and Mom saves them from the trash. She's tucked them away, like she's always hoped that someday I would finally want to show them—to someone.

She pulls the boxes out feverishly, one after another, setting them aside. She doesn't slow down until she finds the one she's looking for, shoved all the way into the back—it's a really old box. Every bit as old as the story that it holds. But it's fancy, too—with a lovely, swirling "Lilly Daché" across the top. It's a box that had once held a woman's most special, once-in-a-lifetime hat. It's a box that now holds Dahlia's most special story. A box she gave to me once she started telling me the story of the Avery. The yellowed, handwritten label on its side reads "1947."

Mom carries the box to my bed and gingerly shakes the lid free.

I've seen these contents before, but now they hold new meaning. Newspaper clippings stare up at me, as yellow and dry as decaying autumn leaves. As Mom watches, I remove them, one by one, laying them side by side across my bedspread like puzzle pieces forming one big picture. The clippings proclaim, in bold, black print, "Tragedy Unfolds at the Avery Theater" and "Accident Claims Two Young Lives."

Mom picks up a black-and-white photo of musicians lined up in the orchestra pit of a theater, holding their instruments as if ready for the downbeat to finally strike. She points to the man seated on the piano bench—he's so skinny, he reminds me of a wire clothes hanger. "Nick," Mom says, "is Dylan. They both have physical flaws that make them feel small."

Mom picks up another black-and-white—this time a

school photo of a young girl in tight, chin-length curls and glasses. "Emma," she says, "is Cass. Both girls with limitless potential. But they do not feel beautiful. Prefer to stay behind the curtain, so to say."

Mom shows me another snapshot, this one of two young women standing in front of the theater. A girl in glasses and the other smiling at her from underneath a widow's peak. On the back, I find a handwritten label: "Emma and Alberta, 1947."

I recognize that face beneath the widow's peak. I just saw that face. On the square.

Bertie's hugging a book to her chest; the cover is branded with some kind of cursive writing.

"The old story is now the new story," Mom insists as she stands, hurrying back toward the kitchen and whatever it is on the stove that she doesn't want to burn. "It's all come full circle. 'What's past is prologue,' as the Bard said."

I squint at the book in Bertie's arms but can't quite make out what's written on the cover.

I walk over to my desk in the corner of the room. I'm no clotheshorse, not like Cass, so instead of stepping over T-shirts and legless jeans that have been tossed to the floor in a mad school-morning rush to put together a new outfit, I wind up stepping over sloppy piles of paperbacks that have yet to become the building blocks for another piece of furniture. Caster wheels squeak as I tug back the antique desk chair. As always, the ancient thing sounds like it's squealing at the sight of my laptop—surprised to no longer find itself near candlestick phones and manual typewriters. I flip on my printer, scanning the photograph into my computer. I pull up the image on my laptop and zoom in on the book in her hands.

And nearly stop breathing.

In the photo, the book isn't branded "Alberta." It says "Quin."

She predicted it, all those years ago. All of it. Bertie always knew this would happen.

Now, my eyes can believe, too. Right along with my heart and my brain. Doubt is a past tense.

The magic is real. And it's for me.

My room is still uncomfortably hot, hours after the sun has called it a day. Mom never did care much for air conditioning, especially to sleep in. She grew up without it; it still feels unnatural and clammy to her.

Yeah, sure. Unnatural. As opposed to the completely natural way the Avery had magically renovated itself—for a minute, anyway—all on its own.

I throw back my sheet, grab my glasses, and sit on the edge of my bed. I stare out the window, through the screen, at the theater. From my second-story vantage point, the Avery looks forlorn in the darkness.

"Talk to me," I mutter to the old theater. I wiggle my

fingers as if I'm trying to perform some spell. Bring the Avery back to life again. But I have no control over any of the magic that has bubbled up around me.

I do, however, have more curiosity than I know what to do with. And if Dylan got inside, couldn't I?

On impulse, I throw my feet into a pair of sneakers. Still wearing the baggy shorts and the cami I sleep in, I grab the emergency flashlight I keep on my book-nightstand and tip-toe past Mom's bedroom, down the stairs, and out the door of Potions.

The air's muggy. Like the entirety of Verona has just stepped out of a hot shower.

How many times have I heard about the side door of the Avery? The one hidden behind the now-overgrown bushes? Every single time Mom told the story about the awful night of the accident, that's how many. It's how she got in when she was called Trouble by her mother—and everyone else on the town square. Everyone but Bertie, anyway. It had also been the same door she'd burst from, shouting for someone to help Emma and Nick.

I edge toward it, the dead grass scratching at my ankles and the scraggly limbs of bushes clawing at my bare arms. But I persist, reaching through the needle-sharp, dry vines and branches to grab hold of the doorknob. When I twist, I find it completely rusted shut.

Undaunted, I head over toward the front step where Cass

sat, singing along with those odd piano chords. A padlocked chain greets me. I try humming a few random notes like Cass, tug on the chain. Nothing. I try humming the chorus of "Anything Goes." On the last note, I tug harder on the chain. It refuses to give.

Above, the tattered remnants of the awning wave in the humid air and the Avery Theater sign frowns—broken and dark.

"Yeah, I get it," I tell the theater. "I don't have the same kind of enchanting, powerful voice as Cass. Who does?"

Refusing to give up, I circle around to the back, scurry down the alley. Tentatively, I touch the back door.

It creaks open an inch.

I don't know whether to jump for joy or flinch in fear. I push the door again and it gives, swinging freely. It doesn't pop, like it's been stuck in place for more than half a century. It swings, like it's recently been open. Like someone, maybe Dylan, didn't completely shut it as he made a hasty getaway.

I'm sweating—and not because of the heat anymore. I take a deep breath, click on my flashlight, and step inside.

The thick, stale atmosphere hits me like I'm a tackling dummy. I cough against the humid, muggy stench as I aim my flashlight into corners and crannies.

I've dreamed of the theater—of sitting in its seats while watching my mother's bedtime story play out. But I've never actually been inside. I instantly start comparing the way I've imagined it (plush and ornate and grand) to the way it is (dusty and sad, like something packed away and forgotten in an attic).

Thick, gray, filth-filled cobwebs hang like stalactites from the box seats and the once-shiny faces of the theater poised on either side of the stage. Clumps of dust remind me of the underwater pictures I've seen somewhere of the *Titanic*. The old, submerged ship seemed to have grown frail enough that merely touching the deck railings could cause them to disintegrate. Here, it also seems that if I dare touch anything—the curtains, the seats throughout the house—it's all grown so brittle, it'll crumble under my hand. I take a few steps anyway, trying to convince myself I can be brave as long as my flashlight doesn't give out.

Oh, who am I kidding? It's eerie in here. Period. The flashlight only makes it eerier.

I edge onto a stage still decorated with bits of an old set frozen in time. The *Anything Goes* set: a platform is stretched between two staircases, representing the deck of the ship. The stage itself is the boat's interior. I point my light toward two large smokestacks towering in the back. A rotten flag still flies at the bow of the ship.

I take a step closer, hoping to get a better look at the old set. Is there any evidence left of the wild event that happened here only hours before?

Wood creaks under my foot, though; I'm afraid it's soft,

waiting for any excuse to give. If the stage were to snap beneath me, I'd likely crack my skull during the fall, and no one would ever know what happened to me. I'd wind up rotting right there, greeting the wrecking ball along with the theater.

I race in the opposite direction, toward the pit. At the edge of the stage, the wood lets out an unsettling crack. I panic and jump, picturing myself breaking through, tumbling straight to the basement.

Instead, my sneakers hit a firm spot; a cloud of dust explodes around me. I'm still in one piece. No basement, no cracked skull.

"Whew," I sigh, aiming my flashlight across the orchestra pit. The beam licks the tops of music stands and chairs. On the opposite side of the pit, my flashlight hits the piano. Poor thing has been completely chewed up by time; the ornate relief along the top's cracked and banged up, and the keys—oh, those poor keys. They're no longer the same height (giving the appearance of a mouth full of crooked teeth), and the ivory on most keys is chipped or missing completely, showing off the wood beneath.

The lid's been popped, exposing the strings inside. And a new (or, at least, dust-free) tool has been left behind on the bench. The thing looks familiar. I've seen it before—at Ferguson's Music. Dylan's four-needle voicing tool.

I press a piano key. A hammer flies forward, striking a string and making a weird, tinny, metallic noise. I try a few other keys. They all let out the same harpsichord sound I heard outside this afternoon.

There's been no protection from the temperature changes in the Avery. Just as weather has destroyed the cloth awning over the front walk and scrubbed the faces off the gargoyles on the roof, the alternating humid swelter and winter freeze have mucked up the sound of the piano.

"Is that what you're for?" I ask the tool. "To get rid of that funky tone?"

But why would Dylan care about some rotting piano? Why bother to fix a piano no one's going to play inside a theater that has been closed for more than sixty years?

Someone strikes a drum. "Who's there?" I gasp anxiously, swiveling my flashlight. But the pit is empty.

Still, another rhythmic thud spills through the theater. Followed by a long stream of muggy air.

I aim my flashlight toward the ceiling, the exit at the back of the auditorium. Is there a hole in the roof? Is some rotten piece on the exterior swinging in the hot breeze, banging against the wall outside?

I lurch forward, ready to run right out the back door. But stop when the syncopated rhythm grows familiar—I try to place it, thinking, *Is it feet skipping? Is that what it reminds me of?*

No. That's not quite right. But whatever it is, it's not scary, either. It's kind of soft and comforting and . . .

My flashlight beam spills across the floor as I drop my

arm, realizing this is the same rhythm I heard when Cass's dad let us listen to our hearts through his stethoscope. This is the rhythm of a heartbeat.

Muggy air wafts, rushing over me, then withdraws. Like breath.

And suddenly, I'm thinking of that bedtime story—the one that has followed me into my dreams for years. I'm remembering Mom telling me that the Avery died. On the night of Emma's and Nick's tragic ending. I remember her reciting what Bertie'd told her that night: *When the right hearts come to the Avery . . . the Avery will come back from the dead.*

It's true. The Avery's heart is beating. The theater is breathing.

The Avery's alive.

I swivel the beam of my flashlight toward the stage, where I no longer see the old half-fallen set but pristine velvet curtains. Panting in a kind of confused anticipation, I stare as the curtains slowly part. A projector pops to life behind me, washing a bright light across a movie screen. Bold, black letters hover, announcing that the scene about to play takes place on June 4, 1947. And the sound of a train whistle fills the theater.

nine

As images begin to flash, I hurry out of the orchestra pit and into a nearby seat. The velvet fabric covering it is brittle. It comes apart under my touch, turns to dust.

Overwhelmed by what's happening on the screen, I simply tug down the seat and sit. Broken springs poke my backside as I prop my feet in the seat, point my knees skyward. Like I always do when I go to the movies.

Unlike any other movie I've ever watched, though, there are no credits, no sweeping overtures. Black-and-white images fill the screen—every once in a while, one particular feature is highlighted with a brilliant drop of vibrant color. Surround sound thumps against my ears.

A train whistle screeches, and a passenger—a skinny boy with a window seat, wearing a somewhat stuffy tweed jacket—presses his first, third, and fifth fingers into his left leg. "E-flat major," he murmurs as the whistle screeches again. One of the color splashes reveals that his fingers are the same shade as the insides of bananas. Too soft and pale ever to have known much sun.

He puts his face near the glass as the train pulls into town and sees her—a little girl, running alongside, her pigtails bouncing against her shoulders.

I smile. "Dahlia," I whisper.

Even as the train slows, applying its brakes, it still tosses up enough wind to push the little girl's braids behind her shoulders. She opens her arms, welcoming the gusts as the train passes her completely.

The locomotive comes to a chugging stop at the depot. A metal Fred Harvey restaurant sign squeaks, swinging from the side of the nearby Verona Hotel. As the slender boy emerges from the train, pausing at the top of the steps, I see his face full-on for the first time.

"Nick!" I cluck happily, watching as he heads straight into the bustle of the busy depot—people whiz past, their voices chattering, heels clicking on pavement. Conductors retrieve trunks and bags while smoke from the engines creates a fog over it all. An atmosphere of *hurry up, out of the way* completely engulfs him.

With a frightened look on his face, Nick tries to do just that—scoot to a spot where he won't be blocking foot traffic—but finds that everywhere he puts his feet, he's in someone's way. He takes a step back, bumps the corner of a large suitcase, then darts to the side only to smack into an older woman, her younger female companion (surely a daughter) shooting him a protectively disapproving look.

Nick nods an apology. "Excuse me, ma'am. I'm from Kennett." As though he half expects her eyes to swell and for her to say, "Oh! Well, Kennett. That explains everything." "From a farm," he goes on. "The city looks so different. So many people."

"Nick!" a voice cries out from the crowd, causing him to gasp in relief.

"Yes!" he calls through a happy grin. When he turns in the direction of the voice, though, he sees the little girl with the pigtails. The chaser of trains. His shoulders slump in disappointment as she waves to him.

Dahlia sticks her hands on her hips, frowning right back.

"How'd you know my name?" he asks suspiciously.

"I know lots. I promised George I would come get you. Bring you to rehearsal."

"George," Nick repeats. His face twists, like he's concentrating. Turning the name over in his mind, as though it's an object he's inspecting for flaws.

"Yeah. You know. The director at the Avery."

"Are you his daughter?" Nick swallows anxiously.

"Nope. I'm Dahlia. Dahlia Drewery, which kind of sounds

like a made-up name but isn't. My mom owns Hattie's, on the square, which doesn't sound much like a made-up name but is. My mom's name is Gladys, but she sells hats. So—Hattie's. Get it?"

"I do. And George—"

"—is the director at the Avery. And I promised him I'd get you. Like I said. Weren't you paying attention? The Avery— that's the theater where you'll play—it's just across the square from Hattie's. And besides, I know this town better than anybody else. So I can get you there better than anybody else."

"I'm supposed to be staying—"

"With your cousins," Dahlia finishes.

"Yes. My cousin, Paul. He was the old piano player. He called me last week. His brother's sick." Nick's voice gains speed; he rattles on nervously. "Paul—my cousin—was called to go help the family in Oklahoma. He needed me to fill in. As pianist. At the Avery. It was a shock. My older brothers, they're the ones who always get jobs. They're bigger. Stronger. Even though I'm the oldest. Just graduated from high school. And you know, until just now, just this moment, I'd never once realized that I have never played in front of an audience!" He cackles. "Ha! Can you believe it? Never once! And I was so flattered, I jumped at the chance. Without ever thinking about what it would actually entail. Until just now. I never thought of it when Paul asked me. Paul. My—"

"—cousin," Dahlia finishes. Her hands are still propped

on her hips and her head is tilted down, and she's staring up at him through her eyebrows. A look of complete disbelief saturates her face. "Boy, you sure talk a lot. You gonna be okay, mister?"

"Well. I suppose I should be. Shouldn't I?"

"Come on, then. I'll take you to the Avery. Don't worry—George will have a place where you can stash your bag during rehearsal."

"Rehearsal," Nick repeats, growing still another shade paler.

"Aw, don't worry, mister. You'll be fine. Promise." Dahlia points toward the Avery.

Nick takes a step in the direction Dahlia's instructed him to take.

"One thing—" Nick says, stopping so abruptly that Dahlia crashes into his back. As they untangle themselves, he asks, "How'd you know—that I was Nick?"

"Because no one was there to meet you, and you looked like you didn't recognize anyone else. Plus, you had that look on your face, like Verona was something brand-new. I know Verona so well, I can't imagine it being new at all—to anybody. But, anyway—that's how I figured it out. Really e-genious, huh?"

"Ingenious," Nick corrects. "Big word for such a small girl."

Dahlia frowns. "Not so small," she grumbles.

Nick takes a deep breath. "Well, Grace? I thought you were going to show me the way."

"Say! I told you my name was Dahlia."

"Not to me, it isn't," Nick announces, trying to turn on some charm. But he's sweating, and he has to fight to stand up straight beneath the weight of his bag. And nothing about him, right then, seems very charming at all. He tugs at the tie near his throat as if vying for more air. "To me, your name is Grace. Like grace notes—the smallest, sweetest notes in all of music."

"Not so small, I said. The sweet part's maybe not bad."

Nick grins. Encouraged, he asks, "Shall we, Grace?" as he tries to offer her his arm.

"Come on already," Dahlia barks. "Let's go. We'll be late, and George depends on me." She skips around the corner of the depot, ready to show him her favorite path to the square.

From the audience, I shake my head as I watch Nick struggle to keep up. This guy is not exactly the Romeo I had expected. Not after all Dahlia's bedtime stories. Skinny's one thing. But this guy isn't healthy. It isn't the way I ever thought she was asking me to picture him. Up on the screen, he drops his suitcase, fights to catch his breath.

Once she realizes she's lost him, Dahlia backs up, returning to the front of the depot, where Nick has decided to use his suitcase as a chair. He clutches his chest, struggling to catch his breath.

Dahlia frowns as she stomps to his side. "What's the matter with you? You're pretty slow."

"I'm not a good runner."

"You're not kidding; I wasn't even running."

Nick chuckles as he pulls a handkerchief from his pocket, wipes his forehead.

"What's wrong with you, anyway?" Dahlia blurts, as only little girls can and get away with.

"Weak heart."

"Mister, that's just about the saddest thing I've ever heard in my entire life."

Nick chuckled. "Is it, now?"

"Yup."

"Why don't you sit here with me a minute? Let me catch my breath. Think I've had too much excitement."

Dahlia sighs, sitting cross-legged on the ground beside him. She props her elbows on her knees and her chin in her fists. And hums. But she doesn't hum a little girl's song— no "Ring Around the Rosie" or "Pop! Goes the Weasel." She hums the tune she's been listening to during all the rehearsals she's been watching at the Avery lately: "Anything Goes."

The image of the depot fades to black. The projector pauses momentarily, as if changing reels.

When the screen returns to life again, it's showing me the town square as it had been in its glory. I let go of my legs and lean forward, digging my fingers into the brittle seat beneath me. I've never seen Verona this way—not as a town with a bustling square filled with voices and car horns and doors swinging open as errands are run to the post office, to the hardware store.

Everyone's dressed up just to come downtown. Plate glass windows of fashionable shops allow me to see purchases being made by women in hats and gloves, by men in suits and ties. One woman stops to admire the sweet smell of the lilies being offered outside the florist's shop. A hand-painted sign in a café advertises its lunch special: a toasted ham salad sandwich and a hand-mixed chocolate shake for seventy-five cents. Next door, the drugstore displays a syrup sure to settle overfilled stomachs.

And there it is: the Avery, still both playing the latest movies and hosting community theater productions. The Avery—the center and heartbeat of Verona, Missouri.

In front of the old theater, a young woman smiles as she pulls her head out from underneath the hood of a '39 Plymouth. When her face fills the screen, I recognize her, too: it's Emma.

"What do you think, Dad?" she asks.

Like she needs an answer. The man who's staring at her is already smiling so broadly, the hairs of his dark mustache are completely mussed, like a hairdo in the midst of a windstorm.

"Humming. Like I knew it would be. We'd never have a car if it wasn't for you," he says. "What was wrong with it?"

"Loose distributor wire." Emma drops the hood with a final-sounding thud. She uses a clean spot on the back of her wrist to hoist her unbearably thick glasses up her nose. Those horn-rimmed specs eclipse everything, work like a fun-house mirror, distorting her features, giving her the giant eyes of a frog.

"Not a problem you can't solve." Her father beams. "Not if you look at it long enough."

Emma opens the driver's-side door and leans around the wheel, trying her best not to get her grease-splattered coveralls on the mohair seats. She pulls the key from the ignition, shuts the door behind her.

As she leans forward, reaching for the wrench she intends to drop back into the toolbox, a rolled-up magazine falls from her back pocket.

The June 1947 issue of *Love Fiction Monthly* hits the ground, exposing the cartoonish drawing of a blond woman on the cover, her eyes lowered to ecstasy-drenched slits, her red lips puckered for a kiss. Emma drops the wrench and snatches up the magazine, curling it into a roll and returning it to her back pocket, her face as red as a hot barbecue coal.

George laughs softly. He's seen Emma's magazine. "Oh, I'm so glad that's the only thought you ever give to romance." As though his daughter should forever remain above silly fantasies of love.

But does anyone, really? Sitting there in the theater, with the Avery's heart thumping in my ears, I can feel Emma's long-held wish to star in her own *Love Fiction Monthly* issue. Romance wasn't something the first female valedictorian of Verona High could study for. It was something that could only be experienced firsthand. And with no man in her life, the only way for Emma to feel love was vicariously. Her face betrays her attempt to disguise her thoughts. She aches to know what it's like to be kissed. To hold a man's hand.

"Got another job for you," George announces.

"What's that?" Emma asks, shoving the magazine farther down into her large back pocket.

"Geraldine quit."

"Qui—quit? But—she—" Emma takes a step forward, accidentally slipping her right toe into the giant cuff of her left pant leg. She tips forward, tumbling straight for the skin-shredding gravel at the front of the car.

George's hands break her fall. In a swift motion, he straightens her up.

"You'd think you'd done that before," Emma mutters sarcastically, pushing her glasses up her nose again.

I'd been waiting for some sign of Emma's awkward ways. Mom often told me that the bat-blind thing had been known for her clumsiness, her unsteady feet. Little Dahlia had seen it with her own eyes, and knew it had been legendary at Verona High, the stuff of well-meaning jokes. *She can fall around corners, that Emma Hastings.* Apparently, it was no exaggeration.

"The musical," George reminds Emma. "Geraldine quit. That means you're up, understudy. Finally, I get you on the stage. I never thought it would happen."

"Geraldine's engaged, isn't she?" Emma asks in a disciplined tone while rubbing her greasy hands with a likewise greasy rag.

George's mustache droops as he detects something decidedly unhappy in her voice. "You want the part—don't you?"

"Of course!" But she screeches her answer—it's overeager, a little too willing. It sounds as though she's far more interested in pleasing her father than she is in being the star of his musical.

"Rehearsals in two," George announces. Emma gasps, letting her eyes travel over his clothing. And she grimaces, realizing that he should never have had to make this announcement. He's already dressed for rehearsals, in a three-piece suit, the shine of pomade in his mustache, the glisten of polish on his watch fob.

"Why didn't you tell me sooner?" Emma glances down at her baggy coveralls. She rubs her greasy hands even harder. "I should clean up. Change."

"No need for all that," George tells her. "Everyone's starting to arrive."

Emma whimpers pitifully as her father drags her down

the front walk. They stand at the door, greeting the Verona players.

On the far side of the square, Emma sees them: Nick and Dahlia. "Who—" she starts.

"I sent Dahlia to the station to get our new piano player," George answers.

"You did what? Sent a little girl to get him? And he's coming now? Today? And I look like this?"

"Oh, Emma. Don't make a fuss."

"Don't you think a professional musician expects to be treated as a professional?" That time, her voice borders on sounding like a growl.

"No need to make this a bigger deal than it is."

Emma pushes her glasses back up onto her face, leaving a smear of grease behind. "What's the poor guy's name, anyway?"

"Nick, I believe."

"Nick," she mutters. "Poor Nick."

"Don't you think that a musician who's just accepted his first paying gig might feel a tad bit nervous? And don't you think that young man might also want something—anything—to calm those nerves?"

Emma nods, her face relaxing into the tiniest smile. "Nothing as disarming as a child."

"Your old man might have a few tricks up his sleeve," George says, offering her a wink.

Emma leans toward her father to confess, "I hadn't expected someone so young. He looks my age."

"Yes." George frowns. "Awfully young."

Dahlia pushes Nick down the front walk, straight toward George and Emma. "Hey, George! I brought 'im. Told you I could do it. You can always count on me."

She sticks her stomach out and smooths a sunset-pink cloth dahlia into the sash of her blue plaid dress. "I'm good at lots of things. See how pretty the flower still looks? After being around all the smoke from the train even!"

"I never had any doubts about Nick. And you're doing quite an impressive job there, too," George praises, pointing at the cloth flower.

I smile from my auditorium seat, instantly remembering how Mom had often laughed, telling me (usually around the time of her birthday) about how much she hated being little. How being a child was something she couldn't wait to kick off—like shoes that pinched. How she hated the way her mother slapped her hands when she reached for the grown-up lady stuff in Hattie's: white gloves (which her mother always said she dirtied too quickly), or purses (which her mother liked to remind her she lost less than ten minutes after slipping a strap over her shoulder), or hats (which her mother claimed always came back from Dahlia's outings looking like a herd of elephants had trampled on them).

"This flower came from a real grown woman's hat,"

Dahlia informs Emma, who's staring at the new musician and still trying to wipe her hands clean. "Mom didn't want me to have it. She said I'd mess it up. But that's what she knows. I'm perfectly capable of taking care of grown-up things. I'll show her. I'll keep the flower clean and perfect. I'm very grown-up. Just watch. I promised her. Isn't that what grown-ups do? They make promises. And keep them."

Emma chuckles halfheartedly. She sucks in a deep breath, bringing her eyes to meet Nick's.

At that moment, I'm seeing them as they really were. Not as the newspaper clipping or Mom's old bedtime stories described them. I'm seeing them as real people, flaws and all: Nick with his pale, sweaty face, his wheezing shortness of breath. Emma with her dirty coveralls and her greasy face and her big glasses, twittering in her gawky way.

As Nick takes a step closer, Emma shoves her *Love Fiction Monthly* even deeper into her pocket.

Across the square, Bertie clutches her journal and points at the sky. "Talking," she insists. She turns to look directly through the screen—right at me. I shiver, straightening my back. My eyes swell. "The skies are talking," Bertie goes on, "just like I'm talking to you. Right now. And they're telling me what's going to happen. I know what's about to go on. Just watch. You'll see it, too."

As she turns and races toward the Avery, the bustling square leaves a giant circle of space around her. No one even glances toward the young girl they refer to as Crazy Bertie. She's invisible.

Nick leans forward, offering George his sweaty palm. They shake while Dahlia continues to smooth her cloth flower.

"Look!" Bertie shouts at me as Nick offers his hand to Emma, who is raising her own dirty hand apologetically. "Don't take your eyes off the screen!"

At the moment their skin touches, a white electric flash zips between their fingertips.

A spark.

ten

The projector stops ticking behind me. The curtains fall across the front of the stage at the same moment that the screen goes black.

I want another scene. Want this to be simply another changing reel. I stay glued to my chair, staring at the front of the theater, begging silently for the screen to come back to life.

One last muggy breeze—an exhale from the Avery—drags itself across my skin.

The Avery's heart stops beating. Silence attacks my ears.

"Hello?" I try.

No answer. The Avery is still, dark, and empty.

I flick my flashlight back on. The curtains are no longer pulled; instead, the old *Anything Goes* set is once again center stage.

I stand, make my way back into the pit, then toward the steps along the side of the stage. The light from my flashlight bounces about as I climb. The set now appears to be in far worse shape than it was when I walked in. One of the short staircases in the set has collapsed; it's on its side. The platform that represents the deck of the ship has toppled, too, and is left standing at a forty-five-degree angle.

"Did this happen on the stage?" Bertie always asks in Dahlia's bedtime story.

"Yes," Dahlia always whispers.

I shiver at the stark scene, illuminated only by the beam of my flashlight—the site where Nick and Emma died. Though the set suddenly appears to be ravaged by time, the emotions here are as raw as ever, locked in the air above the stage. I can feel it all: desperation for love, fear of being found, final pain. I can hear Dahlia's screams. George's footsteps as he raced for help.

Overcome by my own emotions, my footsteps begin to thunder, too. I'm racing, trying to get away. The minute I hit the alley, the back door slams behind me. I hurry through the tranquil night, toward the center of the square. The front of the Avery is dark.

Stars start slipping across the sky. Flittering as though propelled by wings.

I shudder as the stars settle in a clump. One at a time, they move, arranging themselves like game pieces. Forming a large X.

"Star-crossed," I mutter.

But who are the stars talking about? Emma and Nick? Or a pair of someones who have not yet met their fate?

"Who?" I ask, my face still turned skyward.

In response, a single yellow-green flame rises from the horizon, streaking through the sky like the stroke made by an invisible pen.

The streak slowly fades; the black sky returns. The stars twinkle, no longer arranged in any order.

Still, though, the skies are talking—like Bertie always said they did. They're telling a story.

And right now, I'm the only one who really knows they are—like Bertie was the only one who heard it all those years ago.

Starting now, it's up to me to figure out what the skies are trying to say.

eleven

My Avery encounter leads to a fitful night—technically, by the time I get back home, it's already tomorrow, already an a.m. Sleep must finally knock me out shortly before dawn, though. Because when my alarm goes off, my eyes fly open to find the apartment strangely still. No Mom— I've slept straight through her usual dressing and cooking and rushing around. The only explanation for where she's gone is a note taped to the fridge: "Errand. See you in class! Oatmeal on the stove!"

I chuckle. In Mom's world, no school day is allowed to begin without oats. Not some crummy cereal, which is in no way a proper breakfast. Oats. Two strips of bacon. OJ. Without fail. Seems strange, though, that something as boring and common as oatmeal could still be part of daily life. Especially after what

I've witnessed: a movie that was never actually filmed playing out on a screen in a theater that has not had a projectionist inside it for more than half a century, and stars realigning themselves, and the heart of the Avery beating again.

But the entire morning is filled with just that—ordinariness. Even in this magical world, there are still inane things like wrinkles in T-shirts. And a widow's peak that refuses to lie down in any styleable way. And carpooling, which means it's my turn to go get Cass. Same old Monday-Wednesday-Fridayness. A clicking seat belt and turn signals and a really old 2000 Mercury Sable that never starts the first time I crank the ignition. I struggle to get the car to kick over as the Avery looms in my rearview.

Instead of driving straight to Cass's place, I take a slight detour down a side street, toward the old train depot that's shouting distance from the square. Closed for more than three decades, it now looks like another part of the ghost town that Verona is becoming, with crumbling concrete steps and rusted railings. Weather has stripped all the paint from the main building, exposing the wood beneath—in some places, boards are sun bleached nearly white, and in others they're black with rot. The adjoining Verona Hotel is likewise falling apart. Its Fred Harvey restaurant sign, with the bright, white, cursive letters that had once welcomed hungry travelers and souvenir hunters, now screeches in the wind, rusted and nearly illegible.

I close my eyes, reliving last night's movie in the Avery.

Listening to the excited shouts of travelers embarking on new journeys, eager to escape the humdrum.

I crack my eyes back open again. The coldness of decay causes me to shiver.

The dashboard clock tells me I'm running behind. I sigh, turning the car around. Cass will start texting soon: Where r u???

The Montgomery house is the polar opposite of the tiny, above-Potions apartment. The thing's enormous—their basement even has a small kitchen off to the side of an entertainment area, complete with a pool table and wide-screen TV. It seems like they live in two houses—one stacked on top of the other. So much space for three people. One of these days, I'm going to ask Cass if she ever winds up walking around aimlessly, going from room to room, unable to find her parents, like some kid separated from her folks at a shopping mall.

I take a shortcut down the old highway that runs parallel to the interstate, where there's no danger of being pulled over for allowing the gas pedal to do a little making out with the floorboard. Ten minutes later I'm ringing the bell; her mother's swinging the door open. She's wearing her daily accessory: a corsage, pinned to the left side of a short-sleeved powder-blue blouse. Which probably seems a little nuts for any random, not-special weekday morning—at least, for anyone other than a florist. She has her black leather hobo bag slung over her shoulder and keys in her hand. "Good. You're here. She's having a bit of a wardrobe meltdown this morning. Go tell her whatever she's wearing is great, will you? You'll both be late—like I'm about to be."

She waves and scurries down the front walk, trailing the sweet smell of roses.

I race through the thirty or so miles of house, heading up to Cass's room.

If I were practicing analogies for the old SATs, I'd have to say that books are to my room what vinyl albums are to Cass's. She's created her own shelving out of old plastic milk crates and has filled them all with vintage Broadway cast recordings. The albums completely conceal the walls; I know her bedroom's purple, but only because I was with Cass when she chose the paint color from a hardware store sample. By now, not an inch of the paint remains in view. I figure her stacks of vinyl will someday even wind up covering the windows.

This morning she's playing her *Rocky Horror Picture Show* soundtrack—"The Time Warp" blares through her speakers. Her enormous Labrador-bloodhound mix, Jerry Orbach, snores from the middle of her bed. Only Jerry could snooze through the ear-splitting chorus. He's grown up listening to Cass's seven-million-decibel soundtracks—usually while Cass belts out the lyrics herself. It always seems like he's trained himself to tune it all out, the same way he's been trained to bark at the back door when he needs to go out.

"The Time Warp," though, is a strange morning choice. I wonder—did something happen to her last night, too?

When she sees me, Cass lifts the needle from the spinning album. "Hey," she greets me. "'Bout time."

"Your mom said you were in need of a personal stylist intervention. Don't look it, though. That's cute," I say, pointing at her denim capri pants with the thick cuffs, the white round-necked shirt with ruching along the sides, and sleeves that come down just below the elbows. It has a decided sixties vibe going for it.

"I'm trying to find a scarf. . . ." Her voice trails as she squats and starts to rifle through a storage container of vintage scarves, sending flashes of color flying.

Named after the Broadway star, Jerry Orbach lets out a throaty groan as I sit on the bed next to him. He's beginning to get a little gray, like the real-life Jerry Orbach, who shows up in late-night cable airings of *Dirty Dancing* and *Law & Order*. He lifts his front paw, inviting me to rub his belly.

As I scratch—and as Cass digs through her scarves—I'm dying to bring up yesterday afternoon. But I have no idea how to even begin. Do I tell her that I saw her on the steps? That I heard her out there singing?

Jerry Orbach rolls, exposing an album he's been sleeping on: *The Fantasticks.* I smile, wrenching it out from under him. At first, I just think it's funny. Jerry Orbach lying on a picture of—you know. Jerry Orbach. Who was in the original

Fantasticks cast. But then I realize this is my in. "Isn't this show kind of a take-off on *Romeo and Juliet*?" I hold my breath, waiting for her answer.

She glances over her shoulder. "Sort of. The parents want their kids to get together, so they figure if they act like they're feuding and don't want them to, they will. Kind of reverse star-crossing."

My stomach does one of those flips it performs when I'm going way too fast over the top curve of a hill. "What'd you say?"

"You know—Romeo and Juliet were star-crossed lovers. Outside forces were in their way. So it's set up to make it look like those kids are star-crossed—so they'll fall in love . . . kinda like reverse psychology. But with star-crossing."

I stare into Jerry Orbach's gray snout and brown eyes. I swear he raises an eyebrow.

"Do you ever think about what it's like?" I ask, swiveling my eyes back to the front of the album.

"What what's like?"

"Being with somebody. A couple. You know—a love story."

Cass shrugs. "What for?"

The way she stiffens up makes me think I'm on to something. "Have you ever kissed anybody yet? That you haven't told me about? Like really kissed?"

Cass pauses. Shakes her head. "Truth or Dare's a little bit

too deep for me this early in the morning."

"I kissed Matt Fredericks in the seventh grade. We were on that field trip—when you were home sick, remember? We stopped at a Pizza Hut for lunch. It happened by the soda dispenser."

"What?" Cass looks mortally offended. "You never told me that."

I shrug. "I never told anybody."

"Yeah, but you're supposed to tell me everything. You're my best friend. It's in your job description."

"I think I made the same impression on him as the pair of socks he wore on the second Thursday of March back in the fourth grade. And it was about the same for me."

Cass laughs, returning to her scarf search.

"I used to think—back when it happened—even though it didn't . . . I used to think it still counted. First kiss—*ca-ching!*" I say, making the sound of a register cashing in.

Cass rolls her eyes. "*Ca-ching?*" She groans.

I ignore her. "A kiss is a kiss, right? Only, now, I kind of think maybe it's not. Maybe a rotten kiss is the same as no kiss at all. What do you think?"

"I dunno," Cass says quietly. "What's with you, Quin?"

When I just stare, she finally says, "Maybe the best kisses are the ones you imagine. Maybe, if you only imagined kissing Matt Fredericks, it would have been the best kiss of all time. I mean, nobody fantasizes about disappointments, right?

Maybe the best love stories are the ones you make up. Maybe that's why we all go to the movies and read books and listen to the same cheesy love songs over and over. Maybe the best stories are the ones that play out in the theater of your mind."

My scalp tightens and I stop breathing. The theater of the mind. The magic of the theater. The Avery. This is my chance to say something about her singing yesterday. About how I heard it. About the way the Avery changed. About what I saw last night.

But Cass doesn't give me a chance. She lunges toward a small round radio—one of those space-age-looking things from the seventies—and turns up the volume. "Ooh, have you ever listened to this station? They play really good old stuff."

I turn my eyes down, toward Jerry Orbach. He has no advice for me.

A song fades, and the DJ begins to blabber. Cass finally finds her scarf. It's covered in cartoon drawings of the Beatles—the way they looked in that *Yellow Submarine* movie. She drapes it over the top of her head and ties the ends together under her left ear. When she finishes, the knot somehow resembles a rose—something I could never manage, not in a hundred years of trying. But now that the knot's tied, she's already reaching for her backpack, and then we'll both be heading out the door. And my opportunity will be completely shot.

"Cass," I blurt. "Yesterday—"

But I stop midsentence when the DJ announces, "Verona

High's drama teacher, Dahlia Drewery, visited us at the station earlier this morning . . ."

Cass and I both turn to look at her radio as though it's another person in the room. So this is where Mom went. Cass turns it up still louder.

". . . to inform us that the Verona High Advanced Drama class is putting on a musical in order to raise funds for the renovation of the old Avery Theater. They're doing their own production of *Anything Goes*, which was the last musical ever performed inside the Avery. Tickets are available for preorder, and opening night is set for November twentieth—"

Cass gasps and grimaces like she's gotten her finger slammed in a car door. I know what she's thinking: *Two months?*

I put my hand to my head. Dread is heavy.

Jerry Orbach speaks for us when he lets out a high-pitched whimper.

twelve

⌒⌒

"Two months." The words become one of those electronic ankle bracelets—tight and uncomfortable, following my every move and reminding me with every step that I've been sentenced.

"Two months!" Ms. Drewery shouts in Advanced Drama. When she says it, she somehow makes it sound triumphant, like we've already conquered this thing.

But it makes everybody in the class turn pale and swallow hard and start chewing nervously on their pencil erasers.

"After school!" she exclaims, so excited, sweat's breaking out across the creases in her upper lip. "Your first rehearsal. At the auditorium, three o'clock sharp. I won't be there, but you're in good hands with our director. Quin, swing by the classroom on your way. I'll have the scripts ready for all of you."

I sink deep into my chair. I'd like to melt right into the cracks in the tile.

By the time the final bell rings, I get the distinct pleasure of doing the upstream-salmon routine while pushing a metal cart piled high with scripts.

But the auditorium's no better. Oh, sure, when I show up, the doors are propped open in an *all are welcome* way, but as I step inside, it feels like a noose has tightened around my throat. And judging by the strained looks on the faces that turn my way, I'm not the only one who thinks so.

The entire Advanced Drama class is here—but we don't exactly form a cohesive group. Instead, a few are swinging their legs from the edge of the stage. Others are scattered through-out the first few rows. Dylan is leaning into a far wall, where the shadow from the Exit sign falls over him like a disguise. Cass is sitting in the front row as a sign of moral support for me. I park my cart near the footlights, searching for the right way to begin addressing the class. Man—if only I knew a joke or two to break the ice. But then again, in my present state of pure terror, I'd probably forget the punch line.

Liz is sitting next to Cass, still yapping, pulling that whole bad-puppy routine. Yesterday she did something to upset her. And now she's trying desperately to get a pat on the head. *Yes, Liz, everything is fine.*

Kiki's scowling at me from the piano bench in the pit. She lets out a Guinness World Record–length sigh as I clear my throat three times, crack a crooked smile, and clear my throat again.

"Okay," I finally manage. My eyes land on three boys who are seated together in a row in the middle of the auditorium—all of them in red ball caps. And I realize I don't remember their names. How is that possible? We've been smashed together in drama since our freshman year. How can I ever ask anyone to step up when I don't even remember their name?

"This musical. This—this musical is—"

I have no idea how to finish this sentence.

"Might be nice if we had some scripts," Kiki grumbles impatiently.

"Yes! You're right. Scripts. Thank you." I tug the first armload from the cart. But I'm even awkward at something as simple as passing them out—I'm sweating and I'm so nervous, I wind up stepping on two sets of toes and dropping Kiki's copy on the piano keyboard. The poor piano lets out a noise that sounds a bit like a wounded cow.

"What's this thing even about?" It's one of the red ball caps, thumbing through the pages.

"It's about—a boy. Who wants a girl." I glance over at Cass for some sign that I'm not bungling this quite as badly as I think I am. The way she refuses to meet my eye, staring instead at the toe of her shoe, offers no comfort. "Familiar, right? I mean—it's—a common—story."

Then it comes to me. "The title song! You've all heard that before. You know it. It's a classic. Let's get our Hope—"

Cass eyes me in the same way she would if I'd told the entire drama class her biggest secret. Read the most revealing page of her diary. The one she's written in secret code because she's so afraid of the details getting leaked. I'm going to be hearing about this until forever.

"And our musical director," I say.

Kiki shoots me one more glare—just for good measure—and crosses her arms over her chest as she pulls herself away from the piano.

"We have—the music, if you need it," I say to Cass. And cringe at my offer. Cass doesn't need the sheet music.

Dylan drags himself across the room. Remembering the scene from the hallway—and the awful way Dylan lobbed an angry "uuu-ggly" at Cass—the class sucks in a collective sharp breath. No one exhales. Or blinks. The auditorium is so quiet, we can all hear the piano bench creak beneath his weight.

I turn toward Cass. Forget Liz—I'm the one with the pleading puppy dog eyes.

Slowly, she forces herself to the stage.

Something will happen, I think. Something is definitely going to happen to turn this mess around. It has to.

Dylan slumps over the keyboard. He tries once to play the opening measure, but he fumbles. Leans in toward the line of music. Squints. Tries a second time.

And pauses.

Cass has missed her cue. Why wouldn't she? It doesn't sound like anything she's ever heard before.

I've made a colossal mistake, forcing them to perform on day one. It's cruel.

But I'm not sure what to do at this point, other than press forward. "It's okay," I insist, even as the wounded look on Cass's face breaks my heart. "Third time's—you know—"

I wish I could take my words and smash them, sending them flying, bits going every which way.

Dylan's really fidgeting—staring at the ceiling. While Cass is giving me the same evil eye that she should have given Liz yesterday, during the "Dermablend" and "Is it inoperable?" episodes.

Why am I doing this to her? Cass is standing in front of everyone, her birthmark shining out there in the open for everyone to gawk at. The way she's wearing her scarf means she can't even tilt her head in a way that makes her hair fall over it—she can't cover it, hide it.

Reluctantly, the two begin again. Her voice is supersoft—almost like a singing whisper. Dylan lightens his touch on the keys to allow her to be heard. Startled, Cass belts out the next line, releasing notes that sound like kicks.

And she's off. Way off. Flat. She overcorrects, goes sharp.

I wish her neck was lined with tuning pegs, and I could reach forward and twist them to make this whole thing right.

I can't, though. Cass's flush of embarrassment is turning her entire face the same deep maroon shade of her port-wine stain. And she's rushing—hurrying just to be done.

Which means that Dylan is playing a completely different measure. "C-c-c-c-aah," he whispers, trying to get her attention. She glares at him in a *can't you pretend that nothing's wrong here?* way, making his own face turn a matching shade of red. How will he ever manage to be a musical director if he can't tell someone to sing louder or what verse they need to rehearse again? How will this ever work? Why would Ms. Drewery give him a job he can't do? His lips wiggle beneath the weight of the apology he can't get out as Cass's voice breaks.

Right now, I wish my last name was anything else.

The song finally ends. Laughter trickles from the doorway.

A group of kids in choir robes, on their way to their own after-school practice session, has shown up, uninvited, to the auditorium. They're the ones who will breeze through their senior projects by performing their annual spring assembly, filled with all kinds of traditional choral selections. The kids who are not afraid of microphones and speakers and solos.

They're laughing. Each giggle is a needle digging into my skin.

And I feel like I'm being sucked down a drain. Or maybe that's where I'd prefer to be. Because one of the intruders is aiming his phone. He's recorded this. Laughter will erupt again when the video's uploaded. And people from Lithuania will be asking, in the comments section on YouTube, if Cass has ever heard of Dermablend, or if Dylan has ever tried speech therapy. Or worse—most likely, far worse.

And it's my fault.

Before I can figure out what to say, the choir kids are gone.

The ensuing silence in the auditorium is terrible. Everyone's looking to me, expecting direction. But I have no answers. I only know what the rest of the class knows: this musical is going to be an utter fiasco.

"Why don't we all go home and study the script," I plead.

Wooden seats flap up as everyone begins to file out.

"H-h-here," Dylan says, standing and holding a copy of sheet music toward Cass. Even though she's just been singing the lyrics by heart. He's reaching out to her—like a man in some old-fashioned movie offering a handkerchief to a distraught young woman.

That sheet music's a peace offering of sorts. Even though he's not the one to blame. I am. His offer only makes me feel worse.

Cass sniffs, and I know she's fighting a flood of tears, but she leans forward to accept.

As the sheet music slides out of his hand and into hers, I see it.

A spark.

thirteen

A spark. I tremble; my lips are suddenly melted together. A spark. Like I'd seen between Emma and Nick.

Cass and Dylan flinch; their eyes swell a moment. Cass opens her mouth to say something, but she only turns, grabs her backpack, and races for the exit.

I hurry to catch up. "Cass," I call, finally able to make my mouth work.

But she doesn't hear. She marches forward, stopping at the passenger side of my car, waiting for me to unlock the door. She's wearing such a shell-shocked expression, she doesn't even look much like herself.

I climb behind the wheel. "In there. With Dylan. Did you feel—"

"Mortified? Like dying?" she finishes.

No, actually. That wasn't what I meant at all. That spark wasn't static. It was far more. I know it. *What did the magic feel like?* I want to ask. *When it zipped between you? Was it a bolt of lightning? Was it warm? Did the world look different at that moment?*

"But the way you played together—" I try again.

"—was the worst thing ever," she groans.

I chew on my lip. Magic, I think, is not something that can be discussed properly in the front seat of a Mercury. We need time to get into this. "You're coming over, aren't you?"

"I've got to walk Jerry Orbach," she mumbles.

I steer toward her house, but even in the driveway, I'm still trying to convince her. "Come on," I say. "Just come over. Bring Jer."

"Really, Quin. It's not you. I don't think I can look your mom in the eye right now. What happened today isn't at all what she had in mind when she gave me the lead."

She pops the door and starts to run up the drive. Not exactly the laughter and the hug that we shared yesterday outside of Duds.

"Cass!"

She pivots, retreating to stick her face in the rolled-down window. This time I see it—her birthmark.

"I'm so sorry," I say. "About today."

"What for? You were just doing your job."

"But if I hadn't asked you to sing—"

"You couldn't have known some choir jerk was going to show up. Forget it. I'll see you mañana."

I don't even have a chance to tease her about her Spanish class. (Come on—who takes Spanish I senior year? Seriously? What's the point?) She's too quick about racing for her front door.

Still trying to show she's okay about said choir jerk, she waves before dipping through the front doorway of her enormous house.

I feel terrible. Period. Partly because I know Cass is worried about what's going to come of that embarrassing video, and partly because it's my place to fix it. Step up. Become a real director. Get this entire production under control. There's nothing to make fun of anymore if we wind up knocking everyone's proverbial socks off.

Only, in real life, the worst, most bumbling baseball team on the planet—full of legally blind butterfingers—does not go to the World Series and win. Ever. That's the silly stuff of late-night movies.

At home, I drag myself upstairs and through the apartment—which, without Mom, feels as still as a sleeping cat. In my room, I toss my backpack onto the floor. Feel like tying my own copy of the script to a wad of explosives, actually.

Until my eyes land on the Lilly Daché box, still sitting on my nightstand. I carry the box to my bed, shake off the lid, and mindlessly sift through the contents. Nothing new.

Smiling black-and-whites. Headlines I've already read.

Lifting the last picture, I realize that the bottom of the box looks a little wonky—off center. Sloping. I press my hand against it, feeling something hard and flat hidden underneath.

Mom's told me a thousand times about how women used the false bottoms for storage space under their hats, especially when traveling. But I've never sifted through this particular hatbox on my own before—only with Mom. I'd never paid enough attention to notice it even had a false bottom.

I tug at the ribbon poking out. It gives.

I lay the cardboard circle to the side. After picking up a large folded piece of paper, I flinch, bite down on my bottom lip, hold back a yelp. There it is: a red journal with a cloth cover. The same journal Bertie clutched to her chest when I saw her on the square. It appears to be the same journal Bertie clutched in the old photograph, too—the one I scanned into my computer and enlarged. I sift through the photographs and try to compare. Are they the same? It's hard to tell. The photo's black and white, offering no color comparison. And the journal in the hatbox has been branded "Alberta." Not "Quin."

I hesitate, not knowing what to expect. Will Bertie appear again if I touch it?

I tap the cover and draw my hand back quickly.

Nothing.

The journal stares back silently, a single name blazing across the cover: "Alberta." Is there more than one journal?

Why was my name on the journal in the photograph?

Opening it, I begin reading, but find only lines of gibberish. And several warped pages, across which most of the passages are smeared.

But smeared or not, warped or perfectly smooth pages, what does it matter? The words themselves make no sense. Strange rants about clouds and lightning mixed with long paragraphs describing someone named Charley.

I put the journal to the side and unfold the large sheet of paper that was at the bottom of the hatbox, too. It's an old-fashioned city road map, the kind that used to show up in the Verona Chamber of Commerce offices. (The kind Mom still keeps in her own glove box.) This one dates from a bygone era when there was more around town than a QuikTrip gas station and a decaying square. It details all the businesses and landmarks that were around back then—even Verona High.

Someone's added their own writing and drawings to the map. The sheet's covered in cave-drawing-style symbols combined with arrows and labels. On the corner of Belmont and Sunset, someone's drawn a dark cloud in what looks like crayon. Next to the cloud, in ink, is the cursive announcement, "Frank Andrews, heart attack, August 6, 1947." A yellow-crayon lightning bolt hovers over the 1200 block of Kissick, along with the message, "Linda Wilcox, miscarriage, September 12, 1947." A strange object—I guess it's a snowflake—over Ferguson's Music is accompanied by the note,

"Wedding Proposal, Francine and William, February 14, 1948." A tear-shaped raindrop over Hutchinson Street is connected by an arrow to the words "End of Kendrick marriage, November 6, 1948."

All the childlike drawings of sunsets and funnel clouds and lightning bolts line up side by side with descriptions of marriages and deaths, illnesses, good luck, bad timing, and the dates of the events. Next to the section of the map devoted to the Verona square, a giant black-crayon line has been labeled "horizon." Yellow and green crayon flames leap from the line straight into the sky, reminiscent of the strange light show I'd seen surrounding the Avery.

The map needs a key—some instruction on what it all means.

When the bell jingles downstairs, I grab the journal and race down to the store. Mom's home. *The key's arrived.*

We blurt our questions at exactly the same time:

"How was rehearsal?" from Mom.

"What does this say?" from me.

Mom seems surprised to see the journal. She puts her purse on the counter and slides it from my hand. "Wow," she says quietly. "I haven't seen this in years."

"It was under—"

"Yeah, I know. I put it there. Bertie's mom gave it to me. After she passed away. I was still a kid. We were friends. I was maybe the only friend she had left."

"Why was it under—"

"Oh, I just never understood it. And when I was little, maybe I thought my mom might toss it. She never approved of me tagging along after Bertie—who would? I haven't brought myself to dig so deep into that hat box—to see Bertie's old writings—in ages." She carries it to the stool behind the front counter and begins to leaf through the pages.

"Does it mean anything to you now?"

Mom thinks for a minute. "She explained it to me once. I can't remember any of it. None of it made sense enough to stick. Like I said, I was a little girl. Not that Bertie was old—just a teenager herself. She'd been through an awful lot, though."

She glances up. When she realizes she's got my complete attention, she goes on, "Bertie quit school at sixteen. To get married. She was really smart—people said she was always neck and neck with Emma in school. Maybe she could have given Emma a run for her money at being the first female valedictorian. But then along came Charley Foster. Everyone talks about whirlwind romances, but that one—the way people described it, it always seemed more like a tornado to me. Like it took all her original plans and sucked them up, sent them scattering."

She falls unusually quiet, turning a few more pages in the journal.

"And?"

"And she got married, like I said. She had a baby. She used to tell people her life smelled like a flower garden—at least, that's what Emma said. That stuck with me. Maybe because natural gas smells exactly the opposite—like rotten eggs. And I used to wonder if there was a smell, if that's why Charley went back to the house that day. Bertie and their daughter—they were in the car, waiting for him. Ready for a Sunday drive. He was coming down the walk toward them, but he raised his finger and went back in. And the house exploded. Right in front of Bertie. Everyone thought the stove had been left on."

"I never knew any of this," I whisper. Bertie was my great-grandmother. The baby in the car with her was my grandmother. This weird connect-the-dots picture of my family history now has another dot—a tragedy in Bertie's house. "Why didn't you ever tell me?"

"I don't know," Mom admits. "It seemed—well, like other parts of the story were more important. Or—more real, some-how. I was so young when it all happened, to me Bertie had always been—"

"Crazy? Eccentric?"

"I always remember her walking around with this journal, telling everyone about the skies. I have no memories of a smart girl who was best friends with Emma. I only knew who she was after the explosion. When you're really part of someone's life after that big a change, the way they were before seems like a myth. Like some made-up story. If that makes sense."

I nod. I understand.

"Now," Mom says. She closes the journal and slides it across the counter, back toward me. "Tell me about rehearsal."

Ugh. The rehearsal. I flash her an apologetic look. "I'd rather not."

She nods. "You'll figure it out."

"I'd better." I pause, then change the subject. "Hey, Cass and I were listening to her new favorite radio station this morning. Turns out, someone was there bright and early, doing some advertising."

"That she was. And she's only getting started. There's life in this old gal yet." When she says it, she's looking through the front window, at the Avery, letting me know she's talking about herself and the old theater both.

As she falls silent, I pick the journal up off the counter. Maybe I have another view of Bertie's life as she started writing it, but I'm not any closer to understanding how to read it. Mom hasn't been the key I was hoping for.

After the fiasco of first practice, Mom helps me out by hanging a check sheet on the auditorium door. Such a tight schedule means we meet for rehearsal after school nearly every day. And such a small crew—only one class of students—means we have to double up on duties.

Some days we run speaking lines. During which I wind

up telling one of the red hats, "Why don't you try it without waving your arms and wiggling your eyebrows next time? I mean, it's not a silent movie, right?"

Other days we work on sets. Which amounts to scouring through the discarded furniture in storage and the half-used paint in the art room. Our "ocean liner" is actually a couple of old school desks painted silver. We attempt to create the illusion of a deck by stringing a rope between the desks, over which we decide to drape a sign bearing the boat's name. An unidentified sign painter decides to christen our own ship the SS *Down in Flames*.

I snatch it off. I scratch items off the to-do list on the auditorium door. I tell myself done is better than good.

But that sign bearing our ocean liner's name starts to feel more and more like another prediction destined to come true.

I start carrying Bertie's journal everywhere. To school, even. It's in my car. It's in my backpack. I study it through Mom's class as she offers local-history lectures on the glory of the Avery. As we wander aimlessly through two more rehearsals, always with the auditorium doors locked to outsiders.

But I have no idea what I'm staring at. Bertie's journal is worse than trigonometry.

"Alberta," Cass says as she slides into place on the opposite side of the table we always share during lunch, just the two of us.

I jump, slamming the journal shut.

"Didn't you tell me once that was your great-grandmother's

name?" she asks, pointing at the cover.

I could do a lot of things at this moment. I could come out and tell Cass I saw the spark. No—sparks, now, between her and Dylan. First from the front of the Avery when they improvised their song, and later at rehearsal when he handed her the sheet music. I could tell her I watched Nick arrive. I could tell her about Emma, and how she felt so much like Cass does. How it seems like we're another act in a play that started decades ago, that somehow, this magic thing has opened up and here we are, with a shot, somehow, at making everything right. I could tell her I'm looking through this journal for help.

Only, right then, that all sounds a little nuts. Every bit as nuts as everyone used to say Bertie was.

And everybody says it out loud; they all brag, "I tell my best friend everything." Or you look your own best friend in the eye and you say, "I'm so glad there are no secrets between us." In the job description—that's the way Cass phrased it. But that's a lie. No one literally tells another human being everything. I held back on that Pizza Hut kiss. Some dumb kiss that didn't actually mean anything. So of course I'm hesitant now. Why wouldn't I be? This is the most important thing that's ever happened to me. Magic.

I shrug, the Queen of Nonchalant, and steer completely around the fact that this is Bertie's journal at all. Which is by far the biggest omission ever in the history of my friendship with Cass. "Oh, you know. I was just scribbling notes and doodling. I didn't even realize I'd actually doodled her name. I guess—all this talk about the forties. It has me thinking about—well—all sorts of things." I tug the journal into my lap, where Cass can't see it.

It's flimsy. It's see-through. But Cass doesn't question it. At least not out loud.

I still believe that somewhere there's a key. Some way to understand this whole thing. I mean, even the Rosetta stone was cracked. There just has to be a way to understand Bertie's notes.

Completely frustrated, I finally sneak out after Mom's asleep that night, carrying the journal to the Avery. This time, though, the alley door is locked. Dylan must have returned to work on the piano again, and just my luck, he's obviously locked the door behind him. Nothing to do but head back and try to sleep.

The next day, all the way through my first-period history class, I hide my phone under my desk to Google how to pick a skeleton key lock. It kind of makes me feel a little Scooby-Doo, actually, this bit about a skeleton key. But it turns out skeleton key locks are easy to pick. They are themselves every bit as silly as a *Scooby-Doo* episode. So that night I take a metal nail file and a clothes hanger—already straightened—to the Avery's alley door.

Success! The lock gives. Easily.

I step inside. Hugging the journal. Aiming my flashlight. Eyes swelling.

I take a seat. And wait.

I try flicking off my flashlight. Nothing happens. I was sure the journal would trigger some kind of action. Anything. The Avery had come back to life; the skies of 1947 had returned like Bertie predicted. The journal holds the rest of her unfathomable predictions. So why isn't anything happening?

I wonder, ridiculously, if I'm holding on to the journal too tightly, keeping any magic inside from spilling out. I decide to place it on the seat next to me. When that doesn't work, I stand, place it on the keys of the piano.

Nothing.

No heart beating in the theater. No breathing.

I'm the one heating up. I pace. I close my eyes and crack them open again. I turn my flashlight back on and flick an SOS signal with the beam—like Cass and I learned one summer in Brownie camp.

"Where are you?" I ask the Avery. "Aren't you going to wake up? Come back? What's the deal?"

Still—no response. And with no help from Bertie's journal or the Avery, it's all suddenly too much: Mom's high expectations for me and the class and not wanting to humiliate myself in front of her, Cass being forced into the spotlight and not knowing how to make it any less terrifying, and last but oh so certainly not the least of all—no one else in the entirety of Verona sees the crazy changes in the theater but me. This is my responsibility—but I have no powers—I'm not superhuman. The Avery has to help me.

"Come *on*," I shout. Out of complete frustration, I pick up Bertie's journal and fling it onto the stage.

It hits with a thud and flops open. I aim my flashlight in time to watch Bertie's words spill out. Like liquid. They're in a jumbled puddle on the floor of the stage.

I hurry up the steps. But it's as though my footsteps startle the words; they jump into the air, taking flight. Like bugs. They blink rapidly. Bertie's words are fireflies that blink quicker, quicker—then in unison, forming a stream of light. The light from a projector. It hits the movie screen, setting an old black-and-white countdown to motion: 5, 4, 3 . . .

fourteen

As shocked goose bumps spill across my arms, I find myself staring at a new scene. A diner of some sort. And a woman is writing in a journal. At the top of the page, she scrawls, "June 5, 1947."

"Bertie!" Dahlia shouts through a frown. "You've been ignoring me for five minutes!" Roughly four minutes and thirty seconds longer than any eight-year-old could tolerate being ignored. "Bertie!" she barks again at the woman sitting all alone at the front counter.

"I'm working," she says dismissively as she points to the dishwashing sign looming behind the open window that separates the diner from the behind-the-scenes work area. But Bertie's only partly referring to the job she has at the Fred Harvey depot restaurant. Mostly, she's talking about the journal she's scribbling in feverishly. She sure looks crazy—like some character in a movie about the loony bin. Her hair has gone permanently frizzy from the steam of the dishwasher. Her eyes are wild, and the hand clutching her pen is dotted with nails bitten deep into the quick. She covers her journal with her body—like it's a test paper the rest of the world will want to cheat off of.

"I've been seeing lots of things today, Dahlia," she whispers. "Lots and lots of things. I've got to write them down. Don't disturb me."

"But—"

"I've decided, though, that I can only tell people the small things. Because it scares them too much to know about the big ones. I'm keeping most of it secret from now on."

"Do you have any powers or not?" Dahlia blurts loudly, not caring that the entire restaurant can hear her.

"What have you been listening to?" Bertie asks Dahlia, her eyes wounded. "*Who* have you been listening to?"

"I need a spell," Dahlia announces. The diners gasp. After a pregnant pause, the Harvey Girls—pretty waitresses in black dresses and long, white, pressed aprons—begin moving again, refilling coffee cups and sliding menus in front of customers. Diners lurch back into action, like a whole room of wind-up toys come back to life.

As the ridiculousness of it all finds her, Bertie begins to laugh. She laughs at the way Dahlia's standing, at the way she tries to look so grown-up and authoritative. Hands on her hips, a boss-style scowl on her face. But the way she stomps her feet to punctuate her demand is pure eight-year-old. Bertie's laugh gets loud—too loud. This, too, sounds crazy.

"Did it ever occur to you," Bertie finally manages, through snorts, "that there are times you earn every bit of that nickname of yours? 'Trouble.' If you're not careful, I might have to start calling you—"

"I mean it," Dahlia barks, interrupting Bertie. "I need a spell."

"What kind of spell do you need?"

Deciding to try another angle, Dahlia turns her eyes down and folds her arms behind her back. She toes the ground and sticks out her bottom lip, attempting to look extra pitiful. "To turn the pastor's wife into a toad."

"A toad! What for, silly girl?"

"Because she just got me kicked out of Mom's shop."

"And how did she manage to do that?"

Dahlia's face wrinkles. "Because—she's easily amended."

"Offended."

"Right!"

"And how was she offended?"

"Because I said she looked like a fairy!"

Bertie's already laughing again as Dahlia explains, "She did, too—she looked like a fairy, in a pink hat with this gauzy stuff across her face. Why would someone want a hat that only makes them look like themselves? Isn't that a good thing, what I said? When I grow up and start selling hats, just like Mom, I'm only going to sell magic hats that transform the person wearing it. Who wouldn't want to look like a fairy?"

"The pastor's wife, I imagine," Bertie says, wiping tears from the corners of her eyes. "Why don't you use the word 'angelic' next time? That'll please the pastor's wife, and if I remember the pastor's wife right, 'angelic' is quite the transformation."

"Angelic," Dahlia repeats. She considers this a moment. "Toad would be better."

Again, Bertie erupts in her madwoman cackle. On the screen, the diner collectively bristles.

As I continue to stare, a splash of red interrupts the black-and-white images, popping across the lips of a teenage girl sitting with her mother at a table close to the front counter. "Bridesmaids," they say. "Grandmother's dress." "Which flowers?"

"Don't do that." Bertie leans forward from the edge of her stool. "Geraldine!" Bertie emphasizes. "Don't!"

The entire room freezes and stares at Bertie.

"Don't what?" Geraldine whispers. She's a pretty thing, with her hair pinned into perfect rolls at her temples and her polka-dot dress looking freshly ironed.

I remember that name—from the last scene I watched play out. "Geraldine"—Emma was supposed to step in for her. She'd quit the play to focus on her wedding.

"Don't get married," Bertie insists, now twitching and wringing her hands. "It'll be a disaster."

Geraldine looks away, embarrassed.

"Are you *threatening* my *daughter*?" Geraldine's mother roars. She's a dried-up thing, all prune, no more juice left in that fruit. But still obviously as protective as ever.

"I'm only— I'm not—" Bertie's eyes go wild. "There's a very good chance—near certainty, actually—that something awful— The *skies* say to beware. Not me. I'm only trying to tell her what the skies are saying."

No one in the restaurant moves. No one speaks. "What do you think I'm planning on doing?" Bertie screams at the startled diners. "Grab Geraldine's bread knife and cut a lock from her hair, dump it into my witch's cauldron?"

"Bertie, it's okay, calm down," Geraldine coos.

Still, the diners glare. Their eyes are the knives.

After the awkward silence goes on long enough to feel sharp—almost dangerous—Bertie grabs her purse and her journal. "Clock me out for the day," she barks angrily, and bolts, with Dahlia at her heels.

"As though I have any control over those things," Bertie snorts, stomping through the square, down the alley behind the Avery. "Are they all simpleminded? Don't they know there are things in the world beyond our control?" Her heels strike like hammers against the concrete sidewalk.

"Slow down!" Dahlia cries out. "You're going too fast.

You're hard to keep up with when you get this angry."

"What's wrong with everyone?" Bertie asks as she turns down her own front walk. "They're all so concerned with staring at their feet, they never bother to look up!"

"Better calm down," Dahlia warns. "Your mom hates it when you get this mad. I heard her say so to my mom—and that if you keep getting worked up like this, she doesn't know what she'll do. You and your baby both need her. You'd better not make her upset."

"She's not home," Bertie says, letting herself in. "And besides, it's not like I want to get this angry. But every single time I open my mouth, people act like they're waiting for me to put a hex on them. No one takes my advice. Never. No one listens."

"So don't do it anymore," Dahlia says. "Let's have a snack. Some of that ginger tea and those warm prunes."

I chuckle. Dahlia still prefers that snack, actually.

But Bertie ignores her request and leads her to a sunroom littered with weather maps and atlases.

"Look at all this, young lady," she orders. "All these notes— hours and hours of research." She thrusts her journal into Dahlia's face. "This book describes the sky at different moments of the day, every day of the year: cloudless, cloudy, rainbows, shooting stars. Sunny skies. Black storms. Tornadoes.

"I've been watching all year," she informs Dahlia. "At first, because I couldn't bear the thought of forgetting Charley's eyes."

Her tone softens. "Charley's eyes were so blue. Sky blue. But they changed shades, too, with his moods—light powdery blue when he was excited, gray when he was sick, deep midnight blue when he was sad. Right after—when he—well. In the beginning, after Charley was gone, I played pretend. I imagined that instead of looking at the sky, I was looking straight into Charley's eyes. It gave me a moment of peace. I'd look up and say, 'How's Charley feeling today?' I'd think I could see his happiness, his end-of-the-day tiredness, the sweetness that came out of him when he was feeling playful, when he was teasing me. It was a game I could play to forget for a moment. To escape."

Dahlia's trying to appear interested, shifting her weight onto one foot, then the other. Bertie rattles on, seeming to have forgotten, for the moment, that Dahlia's even in the room. "Charley had curly hair. I loved letting individual corkscrews wrap themselves around my finger. Sometimes when I was staring at the sky and pretending it was his eyes, I could almost feel his hair. . . .

"After a while," she says, clearing her throat and bringing herself back to the point she's trying to make, "I started to notice that events right here in Verona matched up with what was happening in the sky—storms coincided with deaths, rainbows filled the sky along with births—and I began to record it, to write it all down here." She pauses to wave her journal. "Just like Charley's eyes matched his moods, the skies over Verona match up with what's happening to the people in this town.

"I've watched long enough to understand the patterns. Now I know what's going to happen *before* it happens—and I've charted it all!" She reaches into a drawer and unfolds a map, spreading it on the newly emptied table.

"I've had to study a lot of maps in school," Dahlia says. "But not any that look like yours."

I push my glasses up higher onto my nose and lean closer to the screen. This is the map from the bottom of the Lilly Daché box—decorated with hand-drawn clouds and lightning bolts and stars and rainbows. And next to the drawings, predictions regarding illnesses, fights over land, weddings, births, deaths.

"We always talk about trying to predict the weather. But Dahlia, we've got it backward. The weather is doing the predicting. It warns us—and guides us. It says what will happen next. The skies talk, Dahlia. They tell me things all the time. And I've written it down. This map shows what's in store for us."

"What does it say about me?" Dahlia asks. She places her forearms on the table and leans forward, trying to find her name there somewhere. "Say!" she shouts, pointing at the cover of the journal. "Who's that?"

When I see it, I tremble. There it is: my name, in cursive. Just as I saw it in the photo on my computer.

"That—it's too big to talk about right now," Bertie says. She grabs an eraser from the drawer and scrubs my name out, replacing it with her own.

"Dahlia," she insists, grabbing the little girl by the shoulders, "there are no spells that turn ministers' wives into toads. There is no need for them. There is real, undeniable magic in this world—all around us. The skies talk. They have talked to me. I've tried to show people. But everyone thinks I'm crazy. They close their ears to me.

"And if they would listen, they would know so much more! The skies, they tell us about the future, but they're— oh, they're even more powerful than that! They can do things, too. They can make the future happen. Yes! It's like—it's like those skies are telling us what they're going to *do* to us. And no one will just look up to see it! Nor will anyone listen when someone—me—when I figure it out and try to tell them all.

"They're wrong about me, Dahlia. I'm not a witch, and I'm not crazy. Maybe I'm eccentric. Okay. But I'm right, too. I'm right about sky predictions, and I'm right about Geraldine. What I told her back at the restaurant is true. She should not get married. She will be cursed with unhappiness. It's not the right time. And he's not the right love."

Nervous, unsure how to respond, Dahlia reaches down to smooth the small cloth flower in her sash.

"I'll let you in on a secret. There *is* love in Verona. The kind of love Geraldine wants but can't have, not with that man she's so determined to marry. The kind of love *everyone* in that silly Fred Harvey dreams about but will never have. Not like this. It's just beginning to bloom, but I already know this isn't simply a once-in-a-lifetime love, but a once-in-a-*forever* love. The kind of love that changes the world around it."

Dahlia looks at Bertie blankly. "It doesn't make a bit of sense to me," she asserts, puffing out her chest in a way that announces she's used her big-girl voice.

"It's Emma," Bertie insists. "Don't you see? It's for her. That's who the magical love is happening to. Not to Geraldine."

Dahlia frowns. "You mean that Emma's got some sort of spell on her?"

"Of sorts."

Dahlia's head flies back. "That scares me. I like Emma an awful lot. I should watch out for her. If she's got a spell on her, I should save her."

Bertie ignores her, insisting, "The magical love I'm describing will have the power to change things, Dahlia. Don't be like the rest of the foolhardy adults in this town. Don't stare at your feet! Look up! It's all true. Remember that. What I say is true. When you get older, don't let anyone tell you that magic doesn't exist. Always remember that it does. Okay? Always remember to look up, Dahlia. Let yourself be part of the magic."

The images fade; I'm staring at a blank screen washed in yellow light. But the light and the screen break up as the fireflies stop blinking in unison and begin to flash in their own rhythm. They pull apart, some flittering up toward the ceiling, some swooping down to the front of the stage. Just a swarm of bugs, all of them twinkling and swirling and zipping about.

In a single swoosh—as if having been called to return—the fireflies all dive straight into the journal lying open on the stage. They hit with such force that the book jumps into the air a couple of inches, then flops closed.

I aim my flashlight on the front of the journal. Now that I'm looking for it, I can see the old, faded, rubbed-out cursive letters. My name, hovering like a ghost behind Alberta's.

I pick up the journal, hugging it to my chest. If Emma is like a modern-day Cass, and Dylan is a modern-day Nick, am I Bertie? Another weird parallel in this story?

The possibility of carrying forward Bertie's legacy is terrifying. I haven't said a word to anyone about what I've witnessed. What happens if I do? If I tell this story, will I be shunned like Bertie was?

I carry the journal outside, into the alley. And I stare up at the sky. There's no light show tonight.

Only my flashlight directing me home.

fifteen

Cass is upset when I knock on her bedroom door the next morning. And not just a little.

Jerry Orbach knows it; he's licking her hand incessantly, trying to soothe her.

"Look at this," she says, showing me her phone.

Cass's face fills the screen, her birthmark in full view thanks to choosing to wear that *Yellow Submarine* scarf, her voice sounding about as appealing as the cries of a tortured turkey.

"Of course he posted it. Choir jerk from first day of rehearsal," she moans.

I take the blow right along with her. I've got a sore spot in my stomach where I've been punched. How did she find the video? Has she been Googling obsessively ever since our first rehearsal? The idea of her spending so much time tormented by it, worried about it, lands another blow in my gut.

"Nobody's even watched this thing," I tell her, pointing at the number of views. "It's not worth agonizing over."

Sure, she nods in agreement. She even shrugs and tosses the phone in her bag, offering Jerry Orbach a rub on the head like all is well. But I get the feeling there's a white lie in that nod. So I make it a point to check in on her between classes. Every time, without fail, when I come up behind her in the hallway, her locker door is open, and her unzipped backpack is propped against her knee, making it seem as though she's only changing out her textbook for her next class. Wrapping my arm around her neck, though, I catch it, just over her shoulder: that dumb video, playing on repeat on her phone.

"Cass, quit," I try after fifth period. "You've been at this all day."

I attempt to wrench the phone from her hand, but she only tightens her grip. "People are posting comments," she moans. "They *are* watching."

She shoves the screen under my nose. The comments aren't exactly *oh, you poor dear* sweet, but they're not really the hard-core stuff of online bullying, either:

Can't wait for this!!!!!
Got my tickets!!
Will laugh till I pee.

"These are from our own lovely Verona High students,"

I reason. "Have to be, if they say they're coming to the show. The only lookers are surely the friends of the creep who shot the video in the first place. Turn it off and come on."

"Are you going to say anything at rehearsal? About the video?"

"Absolutely not. You can't expect day one to be great. Onward and upward," I insist.

Only, that day's rehearsal makes me question whether "upward" is even remotely accurate. Actually, the next three rehearsals make me question it.

On the day Mom's check sheet announces (with a smiley face) that we should be reciting lines from memory, I wind up with a sore throat. Because I spend the entire rehearsal feeding lines to the cast.

On the day the check sheet indicates (beside a line of hand-drawn eighth notes and a treble clef) that we should have the title number down pat, Cass sings in little more than a whisper while staring at her feet (so softy, I honestly can't even tell if she's in tune yet or not). Dylan's accompaniment is weak at best, since he's doing little more than chording—skipping any attempt at a melody line. He shrugs off questions from the other singers, merely pointing at the sheet music.

And Kiki—when the class comes in to sing together, she's the worst of the lot. No wonder she was upset about being onstage. She's every bad televised singing competition audition all rolled into one. Off pitch and off tempo. She has no rhythm. She can't even pretend to dance.

When the check sheet flaunts the smiling face of the theater and a note insisting it's time to run through the entire first act, getting the hang of the curtains and the rhythm of speech and of moving seamlessly from one scene to the next, we step all over others' lines and lose our places in the script and even forget, a couple of times, the names of the characters we've been assigned. We are uninspired and look, in short, like absolute morons.

I'm quickly losing hope that we'll get our acts together.

For some reason, Mom shows up to class looking especially happy three weeks into our bumbling attempts. Probably, I figure, because all she really knows about what's happening at rehearsal is that we show up and I'm crossing off the items on her check sheet. She's really worked up, her wire-framed glasses repeatedly falling to the end of her nose as she leans forward to change out DVDs, showing us snippets of different amateur *Anything Goes* productions. Productions that actually came together.

Halfway into fourth period, Mom flicks on the classroom lights. "I've got another batch of videos to show you when we come back from lunch," she promises. "Different approaches to costumes!"

Getting to lunch always involves a little internal pep talk and some gearing up for it—like getting yourself ready to run five miles. The crowded hallways are nothing compared to the consistently packed-tight cafeteria, which is small enough that lunch breaks have to be divided into twenty-minute chunks throughout fourth period—kids from woodshop show up covered in sawdust, kids in art show up with paint on their forearms and clay under their nails, and the kids in gym are always guaranteed to get the first shot at lunch (nothing like running wind sprints on a full stomach of loose-meat sandwiches). I fiddle too long with the money shoved into the front pocket of my bag. Cass takes off ahead of me today—and Dylan's long gone, too, before I slide out of my desk. At the doorway of Mom's classroom, I hold my breath and take the plunge myself.

Familiar voices are calling out to one another in single-syllable words that sound like punches: "Hey." And "Come on." And "Watch it." And "Quit."

The masses are hungry. And maybe a little afraid the rest of the masses will beat them to the last Tater Tot.

The cafeteria is its usual rowdy mess, with French fry missiles and unending shouts.

Three red baseball caps surround me as I fork my money over to the lunch lady. Which instantly makes me nervous. When I arrive at the small table usually only reserved for me and Cass, everyone's already there. The entire drama class. Chairs have been pulled from the neighboring tables to accommodate them all.

"What's up?" I ask casually, as though the entire world is peachy loveliness.

Liz is the first to speak. "What are we going to do?"

"Do?"

"About the musical," Kiki grumbles.

"We're bad," one of the red hats says. "Admit it. We're really bad. It's not fair. Everybody else around here gets to do something they're pretty good at. Stuff they like. I kind of think the only way to make this mess fair is if the rest of the senior class all has to switch departments—like musical chairs, you know? Like the football guys have to make some giant sculpture, and the debate team has to play soccer."

"Do you have any idea how many tickets have sold?" Kiki asks.

I shake my head.

"Enough for the entire school to come. Not just the senior class. The *whole school.*"

Cass groans and slumps deep in her seat.

No wonder Mom looked so happy. She's selling tickets. Filling seats. Raising money.

We're definitely going to wind up going viral. Fifteen hundred retweets the art department scored last year will look like nothing. We're not just going to be embarrassed in front of our class or the school or even the town of Verona. We're going to be embarrassed in front of the entire world.

Maybe, I think, worry could actually be a good thing. Maybe they're all ready to get to serious work. No more silent-movie eyebrows or SS *Down in Flames* signs.

I sit staring at their faces, trying to tell them with my own pleading eyes that I've put out the welcome mat for any stray idea that might be looking for a home.

Apparently, though, nobody has one to send my way.

"We need to make it our own," I blurt. It's all I can come up with.

"What's that mean?" Liz asks.

"I don't know yet," I admit. "Not for sure. But those clips Ms. Drewery showed us weren't all exactly the same. We've got to figure out how to do this in a way that makes us look good while tapping into our own best abilities—even though those abilities are weak. I'll give you that. Maybe we're trying too hard to be something we're not. So let's all go home tonight and think. I know I need to. There's no sense spinning our wheels after school, going over the same material before we have any new ideas. Let's take a breather. Regroup at the end of the week. Anything we can come up with has got to be an improvement at this point."

"I say we do it in the dark," one of the red ball caps grumbles.

"Maybe you should practice," Kiki growls at him.

It's not much, but somehow, what I've said is enough— satisfies them that maybe there's a tiny little flicker of hope in this somewhere. Everyone grabs their trays and begins to wander off, toward their usual seats surrounded by their usual clumps of friends.

Dylan starts to retreat to the back corner of the lunchroom, where he usually sits alone and no talking is expected.

"Practice," Cass grumbles. "We've been practicing. Maybe what we need is a miracle. A magic wand."

This makes Dylan freeze. "Ww-we c-couldd p-p-practic-ce."

"Together?" I ask. "The two of you? Work on the music?"

"Y-yyeah. I kn-n-now wherr-rre w-we c-cann p-p-practic-ce."

He touches the skeleton key bulging beneath the neckline of his T-shirt. I know exactly what he's thinking.

"Thanks, Dylan, but I don't—" Cass starts.

I can't let her turn this down. Sparks flew when Cass and Dylan were separated by the walls of the old theater. What could happen if the two of them sat side by side in the pit—stood together on the stage?

"She'll be there," I say.

sixteen

I t's Cass's turn to carpool, which means it's her VW Bug
that putters to a stop outside the Avery later that afternoon.
"There's no way," she mutters. "There is no way we can practice inside that thing."

"You liked the idea at lunch," I remind her.

"No, you liked the idea at lunch," she corrects. "And I
went along with it because it was just a vague concept floating
around—you now, like someday, you think it might be fun to
skydive. Only, now here I am, and I'm staring at the plane."

"Dramatic much?" I tease.

"Just *el stupido.*"

"I don't think that's right."

"What do I know? I'm only in Spanish I. Speaking of—
Maybe I should go home and study for our test. Or while I'm

here, put in an extra shift at Duds."

"And this is why I'm staying with you," I announce. "To keep you from chickening out."

"You seem awfully sure about all this," Cass says as we slam the doors of her Bug. Today she's got on a decidedly nineties look: baby doll dress, choker, big black boots. The Indian summer has begun to fade, but not so much that those boots don't look uncomfortably hot. Actually, judging by that look on Cass's face, everything feels uncomfortable at this moment. The boots are a minor inconvenience.

I shrug into my backpack as we walk down to the alley behind the Avery. Dylan's already waiting for us, leaning against the back door of the theater.

"Why this place?" Cass asks. "Why not Ferguson's?"

Dylan offers a crooked grin. "B-b-better ac-coust-tics."

"Are you serious?" Cass challenges.

"Lik-ke a ch-church-ch."

Cass shakes her head as Dylan pulls the skeleton key from behind his T-shirt.

"Where'd you get that thing? How do you have a key to get in here?"

"D-d-dadd g-gavve it-t to m-me. H-hhe r-rentts h-houses. Th-this c-camme f-fromm on-ne o-f-f th-the o-o-lddest-t h-houses he ownn-ns. I ll-likked it-tt."

"And it works?" Cass presses.

Dylan takes a deep breath. Those last sentences were hard for him to get out. He's sweating from the effort, actually. "F-f-file." He mimics the motion of filing down the key.

"You filed it to fit," I say. And chuckle. He must have watched the same pick-a-skeleton-key-lock video I did. He nods and unlocks the door, and we all slip inside. It's dark—like always. Dylan's got us all covered, though. He's brought some sort of enormous camping flashlight—the stream it sends out looks more like a searchlight, actually.

"Smells kind of sad," Cass says, glancing about the old place.

Dylan aims his flashlight as Cass climbs the steps, heading toward the set in the middle of the stage. She stares a long time. And then it hits her, I think, like it hit me on my own first visit—she knows this is where it happened. Where Emma and Nick died. She doesn't so much shiver as she kind of shakes her chest and arms, like she's trying to toss off all the bad feelings associated with that toppled set.

She begins to back up, obviously eager to get away. But she pauses when she sees an enormous clothes rack at the side of the stage.

I flash a crooked grin at Cass's inability to pass by anything vintage. She starts riffling through it all, hangers screeching against the metal rack.

"If we're going to practice, we ought to have costumes,"

Cass says, holding a jacket toward Dylan and attempting to lighten the atmosphere.

Now it's my turn to shiver. This is the same jacket I saw Nick wear the day he arrived in Verona. It's in color now, a light-brown summer tweed. But it's Nick's. I know it is. Strange, I think, that it's on the rack with the costumes—but what hasn't been strange lately?

Dylan places his flashlight on the stage, letting the beam point straight to the ceiling and toss a soft glow across the three of us.

He reaches for the jacket; the moment both his hand and Cass's are on the hanger, his flashlight sputters and dies.

The entire theater goes black.

"Now what?" Cass asks. "We can't do anything in here if it's pitch-black."

I squat, crawling along the edge of the old stage. At first, I'm trying to get out. Get to the back door. But I stop when I wonder if I ever tossed my own flashlight into my backpack after my late-night trips to the Avery.

I run my hand along the far end of the stage. Deciding this is as good a place as any, I sit, drag my bag into my lap, and throw back the zipper. Riffle through the contents.

As my fingers bump into textbooks and loose pens and stray pieces of gum, the sconces along the sides of the theater buzz and snap to life, tossing a warm glow toward the stage.

"Quin?" Cass asks.

I want to answer, but my mouth doesn't work. The lights in the Avery are on. What'll come next? Another scene on the old movie screen? Will Cass and Dylan see it, too?

"I think she might've left," Cass tells Dylan. She can't see me where I'm sitting, on the far end of the stage. "Do you still want to practice?"

Cass turns back toward the rack and grabs a hat—it's blue, with mesh that's attached to the center and drapes over the front. When she turns the hat to place it on the crown of her head, sparkles of light tumble down her face. Cass doesn't seem to notice, though; she simply holds out her hands, as though asking Dylan to tell her how she looks.

I'm frozen as Dylan forces his arms into the jacket. It's too small for him—I mean, Dylan's not exactly linebacker material, but Nick was so skinny. I can't imagine anyone from Verona High being able to wear his clothes. Instead of giving up, though, Dylan sucks in a breath and squeezes himself inside it. When he gets it up around his shoulders, a puff of similar-looking sparkles hits the air, then fades, like the gold burst of a firecracker against a night sky.

He starts to chuckle at himself, pressed into such a tiny jacket, when he glances up and his face droops with surprise. "Cass," he says. "Your face."

He raises a shaking arm to point at the mirror poised on top of the costume rack.

When Cass turns, she gasps, leans forward, and paws at her face.

"*What*?" she asks, leaning closer to the mirror.

But the "what" is as obvious as it is inexplicable: her birthmark is gone.

She glances down, brushing the front of her baby doll dress, lifting her boots to examine the stage beneath her. As though her birthmark could have accidentally fallen off, like a fake eyelash.

I blink happy tears from the shadows as Cass dances about the stage to the melody of her own ecstatic squeals.

"How is this possible?" Cass asks, once her celebration dies down. "I've never— It's gone?"

Dylan shakes his head. "I don't know." I suddenly realize he's spoken—twice now—with no stutter. I was too caught up in Cass—it didn't seep in before. But the fact hasn't gone unnoticed to Dylan. He starts muttering what at first sound like stray words—then full sentences, paragraphs. He's talking to himself—maybe he's always talked to himself, silently. I see him, in my mind's eye, in the back corner of the cafeteria, in the back corners of classrooms. Always alone. Now, though, his chatter's spilling out of him—everything he ever wanted to say but never did.

I can't quite keep up with it all, though—his words are rockets that fly past.

I can't fathom any of this. No more than Dylan or Cass

can. As happy as they appear, what's happened is also a bit frightening. They want answers. I certainly don't have them. But suddenly—almost protectively—Dylan reaches forward and takes Cass's hand. And he leads her to the pit.

seventeen

I start to follow, to let them know I'm still here, but stop. The mirror over the costumes grabs hold of my attention completely—because I don't see either Cass's or Dylan's reflections. Instead, I see Emma rushing toward a piano—it's upright, a newer, more solid version of the piano in the pit— tripping over her feet in haste. I can see a full rehearsal going on around her, actually hear the voices of other cast members trickling from the glass. I take a step closer as Emma happily taps Nick on the shoulder.

He turns to face her, his eyebrow pointing skyward.

"I came for a music lesson," she chirps. "I need some help."

"All right," Nick replies hesitantly. He swivels his head, looking about, confusion wrinkling his features.

"I'm sorry. I'm not bugging you, am I?" Emma asks.

"No, you're certainly not bugging me. I'm not used to getting so much attention, is all," Nick confesses. "Sharing your lunch yesterday, offering to show me around town . . ."

Emma blushes. "Too much attention."

"No—that's not it. If I'm to be honest, it's not just the attention. I'm not the one people come to for help. As a general rule."

"Why not?"

"I assume you went to a few dances in high school. A pretty girl like you."

Emma flinches. She's not sure, at first, how to take this. No one has called her pretty before. Smart. Not pretty. She eyes him in a way that asks, silently, if he's joking. Or being condescending. Finding no evidence of either, she simply shakes her head.

Nick frowns; he doesn't believe her. But he presses on, anyway. "Well, if you had, you'd know that there's always one poor fellow who spends the night alone, feeling the coolness of the wall bleed through his jacket. Watching everyone else dance. No girl likes the idea of a man with a weak heart. No one wants a partner prone to collapse leading her across the dance floor. No one thinks a man with a weak heart can help much of anything."

"That's ridiculous. There's nothing about you that's weak."

He offers a crooked smile. "You're making this whole experience less lonely."

"Lonely?"

"I—" Nick leans close enough to let Emma smell his soap, his aftershave, the department-store newness that lingers across the shoulders of his new suit jacket.

"I might be a little homesick." Once he's whispered his secret, he has to force himself to quit leaning into her, to pull his lips away from her pink ear.

"Homesick? But aren't you staying with your family?"

Nick crinkles his nose. "They eat leftover cold mashed potatoes for breakfast."

Emma laughs.

"Really! How are you supposed to eat that at six a.m.? I'm a home-cured bacon and over-easy eggs guy."

After that, they both struggle to find their next words. Nick fidgets, putting his hands in position on the keyboard, then slipping them back, folding them in his lap. His sad expression makes Emma's eyes widen behind her glasses. He meant it. *Lonely.*

"This place is my home," she says. "This theater. Or the apartment above the theater, anyway. I had sleepovers with my childhood best friend, Bertie, right upstairs. We'd put our ears to the floor long after my dad wanted us to be in bed, listening to the muffled sound of all the stories playing out beneath us. I had birthday parties on the stage. Yes, this place is my home. And you're my guest. You're not in any way allowed to be homesick in here. You're supposed to put your feet up on the coffee table and settle in."

Nick smiles, glancing down shyly at his hands. "That's an awfully nice thing to say."

"And if I'm to be as honest as you, I'm terrified about being in this thing."

Just like Cass. Just like Dylan. Just like me. Just like the entire drama class, I think.

"But music isn't like life," Nick tells her, gaining courage. "Screw up in life, everybody notices." He begins to play the opening bars of "Anything Goes."

"But," he goes on, "in music, you can slip up. . . ." He nods at the sheet music propped on the stand, playing an obviously sour, dissonant mistake, adding, "And it becomes a happy accident, one that leads to a richer chord." He plays a chord that blends with the rest of the song and moves forward as though nothing's happened.

"You mess up, I've got you covered," he promises.

"But the orchestra leader—"

"Forget him. Forget everyone. You and me, opening night. Just look at me, and I'll pull you through. I've got to find some way to thank you for your kindness, after all. And besides, you asked for my help. It'd be a delight, for once, to be depended on."

Emma's face stretches into a grin. She relishes this new closeness, this bond.

"Remember I'm down here," Nick assures her, astounded

by the fact that for once, someone might actually want to lean on him, trusting he'll have strength enough to support them both. "Don't think about anything else. Think about me."

"You seem so calm."

"I'm not, really. I'm just telling you what's going to get me through. Opening night, I'm going to be thinking about you."

"Emma!" George calls. "I need to speak to you." His words are businesslike enough, but his tone has an angry edge, illustrating how much he hates the looks on both of their faces.

Emma rises from the bench, but she has trouble maintaining her balance. It isn't her mere clumsiness this time that she struggles with—it's wobbly knees. This is a new experience for Emma—finding out why the women in *Love Fiction Monthly* were always described as being unsteady on their feet.

"I need you to check costumes—" George starts.

When he sees that Emma's still got her head twisted back over her shoulder, eyes turned toward the pit, George reminds her, loudly enough for the young pianist to hear, "You're going to college in the fall. *That's* where you belong. *Nick*," he mutters, shaking his head with distaste.

"I don't like him much, either," Dahlia announces, appearing out of nowhere and sliding her hand into George's. "He calls me Grace."

"Really!" Emma snaps, as though smart-mouthed Dahlia has no business making any comment and what George has said is ludicrous. The light reflecting on the surface of her glasses doesn't hide the rolling of her eyes.

But George can't let it go. "Emma, he looks different to you. That's the magic—"

"—of the theater," Emma finishes. "I know. You've told me thousands of times about the magic of the theater." She shakes her head at him, turns away, heads toward the costumes.

But it's clear to everyone—including me, in that moment before the images fade from the mirror—that Emma's already fantasizing about how she can get closer to Nick.

eighteen

The mirror flashes white, like a blank screen, then begins to spit back only my wide-eyed reflection. Behind me, tinny, harpsichord-sounding notes float up from the pit.

"The pads on these hammers are rock hard," Dylan explains, his words jumbling, like they're all in a race to be the first out of his mouth. "They should be soft, but the humidity in here, all these years—it's like hitting the strings inside with something wooden. Makes a different tone."

I creep to the edge of the stage, the strap of my backpack digging into my shoulder. I push my glasses higher up onto my nose and watch the two of them.

Dylan's panting, and he wiggles his mouth as if he wants to say something else, but he keeps stopping himself. Now that there's been a pause, he's afraid the biggest miracle of his life might have already come and gone, passed him as quickly as a car on the highway.

Cass is standing beside the piano, unable to keep from touching the side of her face, which is suddenly as smooth as a fresh fitted sheet.

"I've been trying to kind of rough up the pads. With that voicing tool. Make them softer. To sound better." Dylan flashes a toothy grin. It's still working. Some invisible voicing tool has certainly worked its magic on him.

Dylan props the show music on the stand at the top of the piano. And I've decided to find a seat in the front row.

"Ready?" he asks quietly. When Cass doesn't respond, he touches her arm as if to get her attention. "Ready?" he asks again.

Cass blinks and nods, finally dropping her hand.

I unzip my backpack, pull out the *Anything Goes* script.

Dylan stretches his fingers and begins to play with a new confidence—as though he knows there's no chance of a single sour note. In response, Cass's back straightens. Her voice is a mix of light and dark and strength and softness. A tone that isn't just one color, but a rainbow of shades.

They hold nothing back, performing with emotion and ease, because no one is here to watch, to offer judgment. This is the kind of no-second-thoughts performance that Mom has heard during sleepovers; it's the reason she gave Cass the lead.

But they've also seen themselves in a new way. They've

stepped into a different skin. And it changes how they behave. This is no longer the old Cass and Dylan. These are two people the outside world has never seen before.

I'm astounded. I need to record what's happening—jot down some sort of directorial notes. I grab a pen from the front pocket of my backpack, flip to the end of the script. But there's no room. I dip back into my backpack, pulling out the old red journal. And stare at the cover. It doesn't seem right to muck up Bertie's journal.

But I need to write this—not notes, that's not the shape my thoughts are taking. Not anymore. I flip to the end of the journal and begin to describe the scene in front of me: Cass and Dylan, which leads to sentences about the Emma and Nick I saw in the mirror, the "magic of the theater." Their stories have intersected somehow, for reasons I can't quite make out. I only know that what has happened to Cass and Dylan *is* magical. I only know that it's changed their own reflections.

And it's beautiful.

I'm blinking back tears as I scribble, the scene coming to life on the page.

As I write, the tone of the piano is changing, sounding less tinny. The seat beneath the hem of my shorts becomes soft against my thigh. The broken spring disappears from a spot in my lower back. The upholstery becomes plush again.

And still I write.

Cass sings.

Dylan plays.

The sconces die, sending us back into complete darkness.

"Where—what's happening?" Cass cries out. "Dylan?"

The piano answers as clumsy hands scramble, whacking into random keys.

The muggy air inside the theater blows in one harsh gust, pushing at me. Like the Avery is blowing me out. Do Cass and Dylan feel it, too?

Where are they?

My shoulder crashes against a wall—no. A door. It's a door. It gives beneath my weight. And suddenly, I'm stumbling into harsh afternoon sunlight.

nineteen

Footsteps shuffle beside me; as I struggle to regain balance, Cass and Dylan burst into the alley. And they're both fighting to shake off their own clouds of confusion.

"What happened?" Cass asks. Her hand is on her cheek. It's bumpy again. Her birthmark's back—she knows it's back. "What happened to it?"

I have questions, too: *Did you feel it when that birthmark disappeared? Was it like a snake shedding its skin?*

I'm about to say it; I'm about to tell her how beautiful the scene was. How I teared up at the sight of her celebration. But Cass blurts, "The hat."

"Hat?" I repeat.

"Yeah." She's patting the top of her head. "I found a hat in the costumes. Did it fall off?"

A hat? Is that all she's concerned about?

Dylan's wearing his T-shirt, his skeleton key dangling from his neck. *But where is Nick's jacket?* I want to ask. *How could it disappear? Did you feel hands tugging it off your shoulders?*

"A-a-rre y-youu ok-kay?" Dylan tries to ask Cass, then slams his fist against his leg in frustration. Because his stutter is back. Surely that's the reason.

Only he's shaking his head. "L-leftt m-my ff-lashl-lightt," he grumbles.

His flashlight?

"Where'd you go?" Cass asks me. Cass and Dylan didn't seem to see the past scene play out in the mirror over the costume rack. Was I also the only one who saw Cass and Dylan differently inside the theater?

"Mom," I blubber, because it would sound nuts if they didn't see it, too. "My phone buzzed," I continue on with my made-up tale. "You know how she is if I don't answer right away. She'd send the troops—"

"What are you guys doing?" When we all jump and turn in the direction of this new voice, we find Kiki standing at the end of the alley, frowning at us under her wild fringe of orange hair. She's got an enormous purse slung over her shoulder and a McDonald's soda cup in her hand. It figures that today would be one of the rare occasions she's come to the square.

"Seriously," she persists. "You're not trying to go in there, are you?" She wags a thumb at the Avery. "It's got No Trespassing signs all over it."

Still, we stare. We're suddenly all six-year-olds who are too young to be any good at lying. And judging by the way Kiki's confronting us, we do need a lie. A good one. Quick.

"I come this way every day when I leave Duds," Cass finally attempts, adding a shrug for good measure. "Quin met me—we're going to have dinner tonight—and we saw Dylan taking a shortcut. We met up with him. We talked. End of story."

"You *talked*?" Kiki repeats. "With *Dylan*?"

I shoot her a look mean enough to make her back down—if only temporarily.

"Sh-shortt-cutt," Dylan agrees.

"Isn't that your Bug parked out in front of the theater?" Kiki presses. "Kind of a funny place to park, isn't it? If you were working at Duds, why didn't you park—you know—in front of Duds?"

She slips her straw into her mouth and smiles around it. She's not about to quit. Her eyes settle on Dylan. She's especially interested in him. Only makes sense, actually. He's the one with the job she wanted: behind the scenes, musical director. Trespassing's a serious offense. Oh, sure—we're not on school grounds. But Kiki could find a way to make her complaint grab the attention of the principal. She could get

Dylan in trouble. Maybe not booted from the musical—it's our senior project, after all. I'm not sure anything could ever be rotten enough to get us booted from that. But she could definitely make the case that Dylan certainly does not deserve such an important role; that, in fact, she would be happy to step in, save the day. Especially since her family owns Ferguson's and all. And like that—*ta-da!* Kiki's dream of getting off the stage would come true.

"No trespassing," Kiki says, taking little nibbles out of the tip of the straw as she talks. "Somebody could call the cops about that. You know. If they were to see you go in."

Is she serious?

"Hey!" Another voice cries out.

All four of us turn to find Mom holding up two plastic sacks—she almost looks like one of those garden statues of the girl weighing good and evil. "Picked up dinner from Rosarita's," she says, nodding behind her shoulder at the Mexican place. The owners still haven't decided if they want to invest in a permanent, nonhandwritten sign. "Cass, you said you like guacamole, didn't you?"

Cass grins. Without meaning to, Mom's confirmed her story. "You bet. You have enough for four?" she asks as she points to Dylan.

Kiki rolls her eyes, tugging her straw from her mouth.

"C-can'tt," Dylan says. "Nn-need t-to g-get-tt t-to my d-ddad's n-new r-rental h-housse."

"Uh-huh," Kiki grumbles, disbelief saturating her tone.

"W-we're f-f-ixxing i-tt up-pp," Dylan adds.

Cass offers him a crooked—yet wholly approving—smile.

"You sure? Maybe you need some hot sauce fuel first," Mom suggests.

"Ll-lat-te," Dylan says. "Th-ank-kss, Ms. D-ddrewer-rry."

He turns, darting down the alley. Mom heads straight for Potions.

Cass leans in toward Kiki and says, "It leaks."

Kiki frowns, confused. "What—"

"The Bug," Cass lies. "It's leaking. I'm making a mess in front of Duds. Vanessa asked me to move. I figure the Avery doesn't look good anyway, so—"

Kiki glares. She can't argue against any of this. But she doesn't exactly have a *Curses! Foiled again!* expression on her face, either. She flashes a look that says she isn't through with any of this. That there's a decidedly fishy-smelling bottom she's going to get to.

But that save of Cass's—it's good. Perfect, actually. I give Cass an approving pinch on the side as we rush toward Potions, dissolving into giggles.

She lunges for the stairs, but I stop her. We stare at each other—eye to eye. Slowly, Cass begins to grin. And instantly, I start to decode that smile. *Did* we witness the same thing? Did she think her reflection had no birthmark? Because I swear I see it, in the single upward curl of a corner of her mouth. I see her saying, *Please, Quin. Don't ask me to tell you what happened in the Avery. I don't want to have to say it out loud, because it doesn't make sense. It can be picked apart. Don't you say anything either that might make it unravel, prove all of it to be untrue. A trick of light. Even if it's not true, don't let me find out yet. Let it be beautiful for a little while.*

And I feel it in the crooked smile I flash back at her. Feel myself saying, *Please, Cass, don't ask me to tell you what I saw. What if you frown in the same way I swear I saw everyone in the diner frown at Bertie?*

I'm waffling between believing we saw exactly the same scene and wondering how many of the details were different for Cass. As we stare at each other, a few words start to rise to the surface of my thoughts, like ice cubes climbing to the top of a drink. When they appear, they seem like the right thing to say—safe and to the point—but they melt away so quickly, I can't quite remember for sure what they were. I let go of her arm. "Mom's waiting" is all I can manage.

As soon as we hit the kitchen, Cass blurts, "What was the Avery like? Before it closed down?" Light bounces through her eyes as she begins to fantasize.

Mom smiles, pleased that Cass has asked. She's covered all this in class, but it's like Cass is begging to hear the story again. "It was—well, it was special. We would dress up in our best clothes. Gloves and hat required. The Avery was beautiful—ornate and plush and full of gold and red velvet. It really was the stuff of fantasy. It made you believe that the finest things in life could be yours for the taking."

"I can't wait," Cass says, as if it's already a done deal. "Just imagine. When we have enough money. And we save the Avery."

My eyes swell behind my glasses. "*You* can't wait?" I ask. *What did you see in the Avery, Cass?*

"It appears as though someone's settling into her role in the lead," Mom says with approval.

"We could start doing new musicals, too," Cass exclaims, already making grand plans. "I mean, once the Avery's open again."

"We?" I repeat. "Are you talking about Advanced Drama?"

"Who used to put on plays before—local drama companies?" Cass asks as Mom flips the lids of Styrofoam containers. "We could start that again. What were they called when George was the director? The Verona Players?"

"Yeah. The Verona Players," Mom answers wistfully. She says it like she's talking about an old love.

"So the Avery," Cass presses, "it's been closed a long time. Since those two kids—"

"Emma and Nick," Mom says, tugging a bottle of Coke from the fridge.

"Emma and Nick died," Cass finishes. While Mom zips away to retrieve an extra chair, Cass throws open the drawer of silverware and starts riffling around. She's always been comfortable in our apartment, but now, as she passes the silverware out at the table, she seems to be taking comfortable to an entirely new level.

"Yes," Mom confirms as she wheels her office chair into the kitchen. "Closed since they died."

"What about George?" I ask, the thought suddenly coming to me. "I mean, he and Emma lived there, right? Where did he go? Did he leave town?"

"No. George was still there," Mom says. Her face darkens a bit. "When Emma died, the theater went black, and George stayed up there, all alone in that little apartment."

She plunks three plates on the table. In our tiny apartment, we don't actually have a full kitchen table. We've got one of those little two-seater breakfast tables sitting on the dividing line between our kitchen area and the living room. It's a tight fit for the three of us to eat here, but we've done it before, and by this point, none of us cares at all about a few bumping knees or even, on a few occasions, losing track of which glass is our own.

"I didn't know this," I insist. "I thought—you always said the Avery closed in 1947. I guess I always assumed—the theater. On that night. You always said—"

Died. You always said the theater died, too. Turned black and withered. How could George still be living inside?

"Poor George became a hermit, really," Mom explains. "The pain of losing Emma was so great—he crawled up into that apartment he and Emma shared and was basically never seen in public again. He would order groceries and have them delivered. A couple of times, I saw the front door open only wide enough for his hand to appear and grab the grocery sack. His mail would pile up into a regular mountain until the postal worker would ring the bell, over and over, making George come get it."

"So did you ever go see George? Did you ever visit him?" I ask as Cass clinks ice cubes into glasses.

"I should have, probably. But, no—I suppose I was a little afraid. Hard to believe that, as fond as I was of him when Emma was alive. I thought, too, that it was mutual. I never felt like he minded me hanging around him at the theater. Even though I was just a little girl. He felt fatherly. Like he was mine, in a way. Looking back, it felt a little like I was getting ready to step in and take Emma's place—be his little girl once she set off for school. Maybe have my own birthday parties on the stage. My own private movie screenings."

"That's right!" Cass interjects. "They played movies in there, too."

Mom nods. "A stage for plays, a screen for movies. That was pretty common then.

"But Emma died," Mom goes on, "and he was different, and—I was afraid of the empty, dark theater, the same way kids are scared of dark basements."

"Surely, though, as close as you were—I mean, you still

did see him, didn't you?" I ask. "You had to have. You both lived on the square."

"I used to see his silhouette in that second-story window, pacing back and forth. Poor man.

"He did step outside one final time. Collapsed on the front walk. I think he knew something was wrong with him. I figure he was afraid, maybe, of being up there for a long time without anyone finding him. Or maybe he was looking for help. In any event, he had a heart attack."

"When was this?" Cass is fidgeting now, crossing and uncrossing her legs in Mom's office chair.

"Fifty-seven. I remember it because I was the same age Emma was when she passed away. Eighteen."

"So then—who owns it?" Cass asks.

"He had no other family, so I suppose it simply became property of the city."

"So 1957. That was when the theater really started to go down the tubes. I mean, with no real owner—"

"The theater died in forty-seven," Mom corrects Cass. "That's when its heart stopped beating. A theater lives and breathes, brought to life by the stories on the stage. The Avery died with Emma and Nick. When Emma's obituary appeared in the paper, the Avery should have had one, too. Right beside hers."

We all fall silent. The only sounds that fill the kitchen are the clinks of forks against the table. I glance across the room, at the backpack I dropped beside the cabinet. It's only partially zipped; the journal inside is exposed. "Alberta" blazes across the cover in dark-black pen.

When I turn my gaze back toward the table, Mom's staring out the window, toward the Avery. And under her breath, as she chews, Cass is humming "Anything Goes."

I suddenly feel more connected to the Avery than ever. The story feels real, somehow, in a way it never has before—not at any point during a lifetime of living just feet away from the theater. "Dead but not dead," I announce.

Mom's wrinkles deepen with her frown.

"What're you talking about?" Cass asks.

"The theater. It died. But you don't want the city council to tear it down. You want to save it. You still think it can be resurrected. That's not dead."

"I never stopped believing," Mom admits. "Even after the Avery went black and the building scared me. I never stopped believing in the magic inside it. Maybe something physical—maybe that can die. But magic's like the theater's soul, isn't it? That doesn't die. It's always seemed to me that all it would take would be a few new windows, some paint, and some elbow grease. And a story, of course. A new story that would finally allow the stage's last tragedy to escape—like soured air locked in a room too long. And suddenly, everyone would have the ability to experience the Avery's magic for themselves."

It's all here in front of me: Mom, the past; Cass, the

present—and maybe the future. And maybe, just maybe, I'm the one who's supposed to connect the two.

But do I have that kind of power?

"Another scene," I whisper. Out there on the square, Bertie said the story wasn't finished. The last scene still needs to be written.

Maybe it's mine to write.

When I glance back at my backpack, my name is still lighter than Alberta's, but darker than it was a moment before.

twenty

I become obsessed with Bertie's map. Why wouldn't I be? The journal's where she kept track of the way things really were, but the map's where she wrote her predictions. I want to know more about what she saw. Maybe it'll provide some guidance. About what's to happen. And how I'm supposed to pull this whole thing together.

I spend the next few days studying it with a magnifying lens. I thumbtack it to the wall above my bed and stand on the opposite side of the room, thinking maybe something will emerge when I stare at the big picture. I scan in the smallest sections and blow them up on my computer. I'm searching for my name. But it's nowhere to be found.

How can that be, though? My name was clearly on the

journal. Why would she include me but not predict anything for me?

And while we're at it, why have I been trusting her every word? Some of it has been a hundred percent true: the sky's return. The rise of the Avery from the dead. But is *all* of it true? Did she ever make a mistake? Flat-out make stuff up?

Anything's possible, after all. For one thing, why would the Avery spark back into existence, only to quit breathing all over again? I'm suddenly doubting my own eyes. Is it the power of suggestion? Was Bertie really as wacky as people said she was?

For my own peace of mind, I need to know exactly how much is true.

I bow out of carpooling with Cass that Friday, claiming to be behind on a history paper, and ride to school with Mom. I bury myself in the library.

In all honesty, the Verona High library is a little slice of ridiculousness. We have far more shelves than we have research materials anymore; the volumes that remain are all turned face out in order to make the bookcases look full. We rely, for the most part, on internet access. And occasionally, we use the archives of the *Verona Times*. They were meticulously scanned in a few years ago, by a librarian I figure had gleefully leaped at a chance to finally have a work-until-your-last-piece-of-hair-falls-from-your-bun job. And besides, isn't the only real item of value in any small town—research-wise, anyway—its old newspapers?

The rarely used library's completely empty before school; the librarian's not even here yet as I sit at one of the computers and pull up the *Times* archives. I type in the first name from Bertie's map: Frank Andrews. And find a listing for August 6, 1947—the same date she scrawled beside a dark cloud. "Heart attack," I read aloud from her map.

". . . in his home of an apparent heart attack . . . ," Frank's August obituary echoes.

Engagement announcements, death notices, all match up with her notes.

I look up her own obituary. It's incredibly short: mother of Nancy, wife of Charley. Survived by her mother and daughter. That's all—a stack of women, nesting dolls all one step smaller than the one who came before. Under Nancy, my mother. There's another obituary in there somewhere—one I don't want to look up. One that mentions a car accident and my mother and Nancy.

In all of it—all these little paragraphs, these "survived bys," there's no mention of Dahlia. Which doesn't seem right. And suddenly, my family doesn't look like a set of nesting dolls—it's back to looking like that old connect-the-dots picture that's not a picture at all, but a scribble every bit as confused as the contents of Bertie's mind.

A muddled brain, talking to the sky, forecasting wild

events—no doubt that was the reason for the short obituary. There's no mention of the tragedy she faced or the way she reacted. She's summarized in headstone generalities: "Always remembered." "In our hearts."

According to the archives, though, Bertie passed away in July of 1947—so there's no chance that any of the heart attacks or deaths or births on her map could have been penned in after the events took place. They're all a part of Bertie's fortune-telling. And so far, every single one of her predictions is true.

"Let's try Geraldine," I mutter, typing that name into the search box on my screen. "Geraldine Fields." That's the name that Bertie's written on her map, surrounded by a tear-shaped raindrop. I pull up her obituary, finding her with two married names. And the children listed as survivors have her second husband's name—indicating that the first marriage didn't last all that long.

She should not get married. She will be cursed with unhappiness. It's not the right time. And he's not the right love.

"You were right," I whisper, as though Bertie can hear me.

So what does that say about me—why was I on the cover of her journal at one point? It has to mean something.

Am I supposed to discover my own heart's desire? Uncover a wish that means as much to me as being without a birthmark and stutter mean to Cass and Dylan? As much as the Avery means to Mom? I suddenly feel like a girl holding a magic lamp, rubbing it frantically, desperate to free the genie before she's worked it out in her mind what to ask for.

I'm still staring at the screen when a chair screeches against the floor. Cass plops into the seat beside me. She's got on an eighties-era neon-orange T-shirt with the neckline torn so that it hangs off her left shoulder, exposing the strap of the neon-yellow tank she wears underneath. "Jerry Orbach missed you this morning."

"Tell Jer I owe him a belly rub."

"Everything still good to go?" she asks.

"For—?" I'm still so focused on Bertie's predictions, I'm not sure what she's talking about.

"Rehearsals. We're still having them this afternoon, right?"

I nod. "Of course."

The smile Cass flashes is one part excitement, one part *I know something you don't* . . .

twenty-one

That afternoon the auditorium feels as tight as a rope in a game of tug-of-war. And everyone's staring at me, daring me to relieve the tension.

I start babbling, "We can do this. Of course we can."

The faces that stare back at me are all slathered with an identical expression. It reads, in short, *Yeah, sure.*

"We've passed the one-month mark," Kiki informs me. "We're more than halfway to the show, and we don't have a decent set, and no one knows their lines, and music—" she rolls her eyes toward Dylan. "What music?"

"We all agreed to come up with ideas to make this our own," I remind her. "Let's hear some."

Cass stands. "We have something," she says, gesturing toward Dylan.

She approaches the piano, leaning against the cabinet as Dylan sits on the bench, props his music on the stand. *We? I think. We have something?* These past few days, I've been far more absorbed in the map. The play had faded a bit into my background. But how could it have faded so much that I didn't know Cass and Dylan had been working together? What are they up to?

He plays a few chords; Cass closes her eyes. And she opens her mouth and begins to sing.

In what is maybe even a more magical turn of events than anything that has happened so far, Cass's voice emerges both strong and in tune. This is no longer the stumbling, horrific voice that has graced our practice sessions. Instead, this is the voice I know—the one that fills my bedroom nearly every weekend and the passenger side of my car as she fiddles with the radio. It's the voice that Mom's listened to for the past decade—the one that began as a cute elementary school squeak and blossomed into a stirring soprano. The same voice that made sparks fly from the front of the Avery. The same voice that filled the Avery during her private rehearsal with Dylan at the same moment that the theater began to rewind, the piano sounding new again, the seat beneath me no longer feeling like a relic of a lost time.

When she reaches the refrain, she sucks in a lungful of air and belts the lyrics so powerfully and with such feeling, they actually buzz against the walls.

Dylan responds; he backs her up, his fingertips offering their own staccato notes to echo her clipped words during the verse. He hammers the refrain, then backs off when her voice dips in volume.

"Anything goes!" Cass cries out, in a way that begs us all to listen. To understand. At that moment, I swear she's singing from experience. "Anything goes"—when I hear these words, I interpret them to mean the awful double takes, the second glances, the pinball eyes that she finally, for the first time in her life, was able to push aside, thanks to the magic of the Avery. She saw it. Of course she did. She had to. She's singing about it now. Anything goes—she's getting rid of all of it: the bad feelings, the embarrassment. The belief that spotlights aren't for her.

Through it all, Dylan's fingers answer, *Yes, I know exactly what you're talking about.*

When the song ends, we're frozen, every last one of us. In shock. Silent.

Finally, Liz jumps to her feet and begins to clap. She sticks her fingers in her mouth and starts whistling, cheering enthusiastically.

I tense up a bit. I hope this isn't coming across as condescending—not like her "Good for you" comment did over in Duds back on day one. Because Cass really does deserve our applause. They both do. I stand, tucking my script under my arm, and start clapping, too. I'm followed by everyone else in the cast.

"Now, if the rest of us can figure out how to do *that*," I say, "we'll all wind up on YouTube for the right reasons."

Rehearsals suddenly become the destination of choice. The place that everyone from Advanced Drama runs to after the final bell. And running is not exactly easy, not in Verona High's corridors (which are as clogged as some of the grease-laden drainpipes in fast-food joints). They all show up breathless. They show up flipping through their spiral notebooks to get to the page where they've jotted down their latest ideas.

Once the hallways have completely cleared out, they drag in pieces of freshly painted sets from the backs of their pickup trucks. Liz hauls in armloads of clothing courtesy of Vanessa at Duds. She trails after everyone with a measuring tape. She jots down sizes—including shoes. Makes notes about colors that would look nice next to each cast member's hair coloring.

And it's all because of Cass and Dylan—their stellar performance has lit a fire under everyone.

Not that the rest of the student body is aware of it, since we continue to practice behind closed auditorium doors. Which means that I have suddenly become the recipient of the entirety of Verona High's student body ribbing. I'm the object of choice pranksters seek out when they need to relieve a little of their own tension, create a minor earthquake.

It means that I arrive on a Monday morning to find my locker door branded with a giant chalk "Miss Directed."

Oh, yeah. Ha.

It also means random shouts of ". . . be sure to have my phone charged opening night" fly my way through the cafeteria, along with fry missiles.

It means I find the narrow hallway leading to my English class blocked by two sets of quarterback-width shoulders.

"Hey," one of them says, "watch this. Tell us what you think. Seriously." He points to his friend, who attempts a silly soft-shoe routine. When he's finished, he plants his feet wide and wiggles his jazz hands at the sides of his face.

"Not bad," I say. "Wouldn't be too quick to give up the team, though," and crawl through the space between them, rushing off to class.

It means I'm stopped in the lunch line to listen to a couple of art geeks recite "Mary Had a Little Lamb" in an overly dramatic way that ends with them both biting the knuckles of their index fingers.

"You guys have no real passion," I say, stealing a fry from one of their trays.

It becomes so pervasive, even the shyest members of the math team feel free to get in on it as two members wait for me in front of my locker, all to "audition" by singing a rousing rendition of "Anything Goes."

"Flat," I say, pushing them aside as I reach for my combination lock. "You can always try next year, though."

I've learned to put on a good face. I wear it like makeup,

forgetting that it's there, for the most part. The truth is, though, that just because we've got a fire lit beneath us, it doesn't mean that we've suddenly found the answer to every one of our problems. We're not exactly picking up the pace, breezing through putting this production together perfectly. A good portion of our bits are incredibly clumsy. Rehearsal after rehearsal, even though we're continuing to cross items off Mom's check sheet.

We're actually struggling to get through one such scene—one we aced the day before—when I stop groaning and rubbing my forehead long enough to catch Liz trying to convince Kiki to accept a pair of peekaboo toe pumps.

Kiki rolls her eyes—I swear, she probably rolled her eyes at her stuffed animals back in elementary school—and finally slides the shoes out of Liz's hands. After dropping them to the floor, she kicks off her own sneaker and tries desperately to force one of her feet into the high heel.

Back onstage, the players are bumping into each other, and their movements are so stiff—they look like blind robots up there. The lines I'm hearing are forced, mechanical.

I raise my script to cover the bottom half of my face. I'm laughing. I can't help it. Kiki's the mirror image of what's happening up there behind the footlights. Trying to force something that will never fit.

"Okay, okay," I say, waving my hands as I decide it's time for me to attempt to kill their collective misery. I carry my script to the stage. "What would you say?" I ask one of the red ball caps. I press him again. "Your words. If you were that character, in real life, what would you say?"

He stares at me wide-eyed. He finally ekes out a sentence that sounds, to me, a little like the hallway shouts that fill the air as the Verona High stream flows to lunch. Staccato grunts. But it comes out of him naturally. Finally. I nod. "Write it down in your scripts. All of you."

"You mean change the line?" the ball cap asks.

"Yes," I say, scratching the dialogue out of my own manuscript and writing his sentence above it. "Change the line. Make it your own."

I return to my seat. But something has happened to me with the scratching out of that sentence. It suddenly sends my mind spinning. I'm staring at the entire scene now—not just that single line of dialogue. And I draw a giant X over the page.

There's no room in the margins for what I want to do, so I reach into my backpack and pull out Bertie's journal. I flip to the back. But this time, as I fill one page, another blank page appears behind it. I write frantically. Beneath a rapidly spreading sense of relief. This is fun—more so even than refusing to let the hallway goons get to me. And it hits me that it *should* be fun. I'm giggling under my breath, pressing so hard against the pages that I nearly tear them with my pen tip. Until I hear my name.

When I glance up, I realize Kiki's annoyed scowl, plastered onto her flushed face, is directed at me. "You're not even watching," she accuses me.

Maybe it's because I've been backed into a corner. Maybe it's because I'm looking at her face and remembering all the times that she ratted someone out for having equations written on the inside of their wrist during algebra exams. But now I'm visualizing everything that could happen if I were to slam the journal shut and shove it in my backpack, go back to the scene we'd just been working on, which was only barely limping along.

I'm seeing myself in the principal's office, in front of his desk, slumped into a chair that feels every bit as unforgiving as Kiki's words: *It's her* mother. *Why* wouldn't *she have gotten the director's job? I'm not one to be critical.* (At this point, I picture the principal's eyes flashing Kiki a look he's picked up from the student population, something along the lines of "Gimme a break.") *But she's not offering us the kind of direction we really need,* I imagine Kiki continuing to say. *She's spending rehearsals not paying any attention at all! She's coasting. Completely. Of course, I would be completely happy to give up my role and step in. Save the musical. We could just switch places. . . .*

I refuse to give Kiki any ammunition. "I'm listening to everything you say," I insist, standing. "And revising it as we go along."

"What's that supposed to mean?" she asks. "Revising?"

I begin to read what I've written. At first, it's nothing more than a chain reaction. Kiki's kicked me and I've kicked back. As the minutes pulse, though, what I'm doing sinks in. And it starts to scare me. A voice in the back of my head reminds me that there were plenty of reasons why I didn't get shunted off to journalism with the rest of the writers during freshman year. I'm not the person who reads aloud from my own work. I don't have a blog where I post my latest flash fiction for the world to read. I'm a closet scribbler, a girl with hatboxes full of stories that have never seen sunlight.

Once I've started, though, I can't stop. I'm suddenly reciting the passages I'd scrawled in the back of Bertie's journal word for word. Every once in a while, someone actually laughs. A welcome chuckle here and there.

As the players move around, they occasionally let out an "Oh—yeah—okay, that's better," and then, later on, a few begin to say, "Hey, Quin, what if—" And we're brainstorming, and the scene is changing completely, but who cares? We're laughing and this feels better—it's a shoe that actually fits.

"I have no idea how that's going to work in with the rest of the musical," Cass admits as we wrap for the day and the class is gathering their stuff, heading for the exit. "But it was a blast."

She's right—I know she is. All the way home, all I can think about is tying the threads together. Connecting the dots between the musical and what we've just practiced. So I burst into my room, and I flip to the scene I've written at the end of Bertie's journal. "Anything Goes Notes," I've scribbled at the top of the first page.

Why not? What if (literally) anything goes that doesn't work?

Suddenly, I'm attacking this boy-wants-girl story, scratching out whole scenes, whole passages in the manuscript, adding new lines and scenarios. The next afternoon, at rehearsal, I share them.

The cast sits cross-legged on the floor, leaning forward, shouting out an occasional "No—it'd be like this—" Or "What if—?"

The entirety of Advanced Drama is responding. It's a collective give-and-take now.

Mom's still off having signs printed, taking out ads in the newspaper, coming up with advertising slogans to be featured during the nightly local news. She's on the phone, calling all the muckety-mucks she can find within the city limits—like a cold-call sales pitch, a "Can I put you down for two tickets, then?" She wants everyone to come out— and she's telling them we're picking up right where the Avery left off. Finishing the *Anything Goes* run—just imagine what we could do inside the theater! Of course we can't let the city tear it down!

Except that's not what we're doing. The play keeps shifting. I'm not sure, exactly, what Mom's going to say when she sees it. But I'm oddly protective of it—it's a work in progress that I'm not quite sure how to describe yet. So I keep all our revisions to myself. The rest of the cast follows my lead. No one says a word about it in class. Not even when Mom asks for status updates. We're purposefully vague.

"Hey! Quin!" Liz shouts toward the end of the week, at the close of one particularly long rehearsal. All the players are breaking up, finally dispersing, filing out through the doors that lead to the vacant hallways, then the parking lot. "I was thinking. Why don't we have the audience show up in vintage clothes? Wouldn't that be cool? Do you think you could tell Ms. Drewery? She could put out the word. It would be another way to get some advertising. We could put up some signs in Duds. Maybe she could get that on the radio, too. Make it kind of sound like an event or a party, not just a high school play."

I like the idea, to be honest. "I'll tell her," I promise.

"I've got an idea, too," one of the red ball caps announces. Toby. His name's Toby. "For the background. I was thinking, why not use a black sheet—for the sky, you know? I could rig it to where white lights poked through. You know, for stars."

Stars? This tickles the back of my thoughts. Bertie. The night sky. Star-crossed lovers uncrossed.

A thump behind me steals my attention. Dylan's staring at his toes, while another red cap—Michael, this one's name is Michael—is thunking him on the back. Dylan's face is red, and he's looking uncomfortable. I'm about to tell Michael to beat it—what's he doing, slapping Dylan on the back, teasing him about his stutter? Acting like he's trying to free him of words stuck in his throat like chicken bones, saying, "Come on, spit it out already"?

But that's not it at all. That slap isn't a tease. It's congratulatory. "She's really into you," Michael says. Followed by two decidedly *way to go* thumps.

I'm wondering who Michael means as a smile squirms across Dylan's face.

"I'm taking that as a yes. I'll get right on it," Toby announces triumphantly. When I glance his way, he's backing up, insisting, "You'll see. This'll be great."

When I turn back toward Dylan and Michael, the two are already gone. I sigh, reaching for the strap of my backpack. Beside my stash, Cass's phone begins to buzz on top of her small tower of textbooks. I glance at the screen as a text comes in from Dylan: Meet me. Same time 2day. Avery.

His voice is every bit as clear via text as it is inside that old theater.

twenty-two

Cass's VW putters along toward the square. Her hair flutters out around her face, and she's humming to the radio, that station she recently found—the one that plays her old faves. The one that Mom visited to make the first *Anything Goes* announcement. I stare, waiting. But Cass says nothing. Not about meeting Dylan later. Not about what the two of them are up to in the Avery. Not even when the DJ reminds his listeners, between songs, that tickets for our production are on sale now.

Cass isn't talking to me. And I'm not talking to her, either. One omission has led to another, and here we are, sitting on a mountain of silence. She's got Dylan on her mind. She's rushing to meet him. She's racing toward whatever's happening to her inside that old theater. She's sharing it with Dylan. Not with me.

I get a panicky feeling, wondering if we're standing on a road that forks. Like she's choosing something other than me, for the first time since those days of paste eating and afternoon naps.

This can't be happening—and still, it is. I'm losing my hold on her. She has a secret. An enormous one.

And so do I.

And neither one of us says anything.

And I hate it.

As we pile out of the Bug, I'm still expecting it to come. Some mention of the text. Something as simple as for her to turn and sprint straight for the Avery right in front of me. But she takes a step toward Duds.

"Hey, Cass—" I call. *Just come out with it, already. I saw the text. Tell me what this is all about.*

She turns, staring blankly. But I can't decode this face—maybe because it isn't honest. This isn't an open, waiting-for-what-comes-next blank face. This is a poker face, a cover—for the first time since I've known her, the face Cass turns toward me is a lie. Not just an omission. This face insists nothing's going on. This face says her life right now is none of my business.

I pull off my glasses and wipe the lenses with the bottom

of my T-shirt. Like maybe I could see something else when I slide them back on.

But no—nothing. Just Cass standing in a pair of bell-bottoms with embroidered hems. A red-checkered blouse. And that blank face she's put on to cover whatever it is she feels she needs to hide. From me, of all people.

"See you in the a.m.," she calls. Like it's any other day, no big deal. And more—she says it in order to put a giant "The End" on this conversation. To make sure I don't have a chance to pry.

I take the long way around the square, walking down the sidewalk that makes up the perimeter. When I get to Ferguson's, I cup my eyes and press my face against the glass. No sign of Dylan. Only Kiki's father, reorganizing his display of instruction booklets.

I try the alley behind the Avery. Still no sign of Dylan—no bike, no half-open back door. The knob won't twist when I try it. Surely he'd have to leave it open for Cass, right? He's the one with the filed-down skeleton key.

Reluctantly, I give up. At least for now. Maybe, I think, they're supposed to meet up later. After dark, even.

"You'll give me a sign, won't you?" I ask out loud, placing my palm against the rough brick on the back of the Avery.

Like Cass, the Avery decides to remain silent.

Mom's already home when I finally step inside. The

microwave is beeping, and the kitchen smells like tomato sauce. Lasagna, I think—one of the many frozen dinners she's been dropping on our dinner table ever since we both got involved in the musical. *Two months.* A crazy deadline. The kind that induces panic and keeps the stove from ever getting turned on, any real home cooking from ever getting served.

Without even a hello, she launches into a tirade on the numbers. "Ticket sales have slowed down *dramatically*—no pun intended. But I did place a few calls to some people I think might offer to invest in the Avery once they see our production and everyone starts getting riled up about it again—including their kids."

Her white hair tumbles over the top of her glasses. "And once we get those investors, it'll all come back—the whole square. After all, what do people need once the final bow has been taken? Pie!"

I giggle. But the look Mom flashes is serious. She hadn't meant that as a joke. "The businesses on the square closed, one after another, after the Avery died. But let me tell you, when people get out of the theater—or leave from a movie— they don't want to go home. They want to talk about what they've seen. They need coffee shops, restaurants. They need a table for two and a little dessert plate between them. Pie! One plate, two forks. Something sweet. They need a sidewalk café in the summer. They need—"

"—specialty hot chocolates in the winter," I finish. "Late

dinners. Then, if the conversation gets heated, an early break-fast."

Mom smiles, nodding in agreement. "We need a florist showing off their green thumb, too. Create almost a—well, a minipark—right there in the center of the square. With bushes and flowers growing up around benches. And once everyone sees what that florist's created, they'll start thinking about getting some flowers of their own. Maybe people could come to like corsages again! Wear them to the theater! Yes! Wouldn't Cass's mother like a flower shop down here? If there was a lot of traffic? Wouldn't it please her as much—more, even—to see people going into the Avery wearing a corsage like the ones she wears every day than it would to make floral arrangements for sick people at the hospital?

"Even the businesses still here," Mom goes on, sliding the lasagna out of the microwave and cutting single-serving squares with a spatula, plopping them onto two plates. "They'd ben-efit directly, too! Ferguson's would always be renting or selling or repairing instruments for the musicians in the orchestra. And sound equipment! They'd have to supply the Avery with that, too. But after seeing a musical, wouldn't people be walk-ing into Ferguson's inspired? Wouldn't they point to a guitar or violin hanging on the wall, wanting to try it out for them-selves? Wouldn't that mean that Ferguson's would need more music teachers?

"And Duds!" She's on a roll now. "Same thing. Sure, Duds

would provide costumes, but then, wouldn't more people be passing by Duds, window-shopping at first, then going inside, deciding one of Vanessa's old sixties-era jackets would be fun with a pair of their own jeans?

"It would spiral out from there—those people who had bought instruments of their own at Ferguson's, well, they'd get to be half-decent pickers. And they'd want a place to play on Friday nights. So we'd need a good watering hole. And with more people buying up vintage clothes from Duds, wouldn't it make sense that a cleaner's would go in next door, one that would do alterations?

"A destination! Don't you see? Because of the Avery, the square would become a hot spot again. Even Rosarita's would wind up with a permanent sign!"

She pants as though she's crossed the finish line of a marathon as she places our plates on the small table. But she's not the least bit exhausted—energized is more like it.

"So! Rehearsals!" Mom shouts, trying to catch her breath. She stares at me expectantly.

And now I don't want to eat at all. She's banking on *Anything Goes* being *the* thing that ignites enough interest to revive the entire town of Verona, and what have I done? I've changed the entire musical—new scenes, new dialogue. I should tell her. Now is the time to say something, because if all this fails, if it comes crashing down, I'll be the one to blame for the death of not only the Avery but the whole town. I mean, what'll happen when she shows up on opening night, and it's nothing at all like the play she remembers? When she realizes I've taken her childhood memories and cut them apart, pasted them into a different picture? What will she think about that?

But I'm a coward. *The music,* I think. *The music hasn't changed. Tell her about that. It's safe.*

"Cass and Dylan are really amazing," I say. Which is true. "So good, they've wound up inspiring the rest of the cast."

She grins. "See? What'd I tell you? People rise to the occasion. High expectations can be an incredible tool. Get everyone performing at their best."

"I love the title number," I babble. "It's really strong—Cass really puts her heart into the lyrics in the verse. And Dylan kind of pushes her forward, increasing the tempo sometimes, until the notes almost start to sound staccato—"

"Mmm," Mom says, understanding. "Grace notes." And she grimaces. That's what Nick called her when she met him at the train. Right then, I see her little-girl features, still there in her face. I see Dahlia—Trouble—who didn't like to be seen as small, unimportant.

She shakes it off, though, saying, "If the Avery comes back, and the square comes back, Potions will still matter. Maybe you won't want a perfumery any more than I wanted Hattie's. But because of its location, you'll be able to carry on, make it into whatever you want it to be. You'll have something of value."

Wow. As if the weight of the musical wasn't already enough—save the theater, save the town—now Mom's piling my financial future on top of it all. No wonder this thing's so important to her.

"You know, though," I say quietly, "you don't just inherit stuff."

She glances across the table, surprise washing her face. When the surprise lets go, I see a flash of satisfaction. I've pleased her.

Without warning, night falls. I look through the window as the neon Avery sign ignites, throwing a shower of sparks high in the air. The marquee lights, too, casting a glow across the square, through the window, my plate, the side of Mom's face.

I can't breathe. Mom's staring right at the theater. I want to scream, *It's alive! Little Dahlia, the chaser of trains, don't you see it? The Avery is back from the dead, looking like it did all those years ago. It's not so far gone. . . .*

She only sighs. "Thought I saw headlights. But who would be driving down here at this time of day? Probably all my blabbering about what the square could be. Kind of getting ahead of myself, wasn't I? Letting my imagination get the best of me."

She doesn't see it?

The yellow neon glow slowly vanishes from the side of her face. The Avery's dark again.

It has to be a sign. I have to find out what's going on inside the Avery.

Searching for any excuse to get out to investigate, I tell her, "I've got a lot of homework."

She waves her hand, shooing me away as she warns, "Don't let rehearsals get in the way of your other classes. Don't let those grades slip. . . ."

But I'm moving too fast to hear the rest. I'm dropping my leftover lasagna serving in a refrigerator bowl and rinsing my plate.

Mom's still picking at her own dinner as I grab my backpack, shouting, "I just remembered. I promised to meet up—with Cass—to study. Won't be late." My feet are already on the stairs, and I'm running, running, straight to the alley behind the Avery.

The door's shut, but not locked.

I push my way inside.

Muffled voices bounce through the darkness.

twentythree

It's Cass and Dylan. I recognize their voices instantly. I press forward, afraid of the floor squeaking beneath my feet. Afraid to breathe and give myself away.

I haven't been invited. I'm eavesdropping. All in a single *whoosh*, I feel both guilty about it and glad to be witness to whatever's happening. I need everything in here—my best friend. The theater. To find out what, exactly, my next step should be.

I've got the feeling I'm walking a tightrope. It's hard to swallow. I press forward, deeper into the darkness.

A sudden burst of light pops behind my shoulder. I squat, hiding behind the nearest seat along the far side of the theater.

It's a spotlight. And Cass and Dylan are beneath it, both of them sitting in the center of the stage.

I'm too close. The spotlight's throwing too many strange shadows. I need to get to a safer spot. A spot where no light can show me snooping.

I've never been in the balcony, but the stairs are close enough for me to sneak up. I decide to give it a shot.

I put my weight on the bottom step; it creaks a little. Not dangerously, but like I've startled it. Like it's never expected to feel footsteps again.

The railing at the front of the balcony feels surprisingly sturdy. I take a seat, swallowing a yelp as I plop down on something hard. A pair of tiny binoculars. Opera glasses. Left behind after the last performance. And something soft beneath them—a handkerchief, maybe?

I imagine a woman moved to tears, right here, in this very seat. Blown away by the power of the performances. I picture her so overcome, she staggers out of the theater, unable to think straight.

What will be the response to our own performance? Polite applause? Or sneers?

The opera glasses come in handy—as if left behind just for me to use. They bring me closer to Cass and Dylan, sitting in front of the old, toppled stairs. They're both in full costume—and by "costume," I don't mean the old blue pillbox hat or the too-small jacket. I mean that Cass has no birthmark. I mean Dylan's moving his mouth, gesturing animatedly, in a picture of complete confidence.

I chuckle to myself. Dylan's suddenly got more swagger than all the guys on the varsity football team combined. Maybe that's always been his great fantasy—a touch of swagger to go along with perfectly polished words—the way other boys dream about fame or passing calculus or finally winning a smile from the prettiest girl in school.

"I could pick you up, you know," Cass is telling him.

"It's all right," he says, shrugging. "It'd seem strange to see me without my bike. My folks would ask questions."

"How come you haven't gotten your license?"

He laughs. "Are you kidding? My stutter gets worse when I'm nervous. I can see myself trying to take a test. I'd turn into a regular jackhammer."

"You're going to take it sometime, though, aren't you?"

"I'd rather stick with the bike till my age flips triple digits." He shrugs. "I've got the bus when the weather's bad."

"At least you can avoid drawing attention to yourself," Cass offers, in a *trust me, you're better off than I am* sort of way. "My splotchy red face is front and center everywhere I go."

"I can avoid—? Oh, man. It's *always* there. Everyone pretends not to see me so they don't have to talk to me. Teachers don't call on me. Kids walk around me. People are afraid to say hi, because they know that it'll take an hour and a half for me to get a hello out."

"People never look at me. They don't talk to you, but they

won't *look* at me. It makes me feel like a ghost sometimes."

"So stupid," Dylan says, shaking his head is disbelief. "It's like not looking at a flower or a sunset or a painting."

"Don't—" Cass shakes her head. "It's a lot harder to look at me outside here. You know it is."

"No, it's not." Dylan says it so quietly, I almost miss it completely. "It's especially not hard to look at you when you're singing. That's what I think, anyway. Every day we're at rehearsals."

"Would you look at me in rehearsal, though, if it weren't for our time in here?" Cass asks.

"Would you have let me?" Dylan counters. "Or would me looking at you make you so uncomfortable you'd have to turn away?"

When Cass doesn't answer, he asks, "Would you have ever talked to me if it weren't for our time in here?"

"And would you have answered? Or would you have been too self-conscious about your stutter?"

"I don't know," Dylan answers honestly.

"You ever wonder why this—change—in both of us—only happens in here?" Cass finally asks. "Or why it even happens in here at all? I'd tell myself I was dreaming—or think I was completely losing it—if it weren't for you."

Instead of answering, Dylan confesses, "I always wished I could go to a school for deaf kids. I wish I could pretend to be deaf, and use sign language the rest of my life."

"Wow," Cass breathes. "Then I could go to a school for blind kids. And no one would ever be pretending not to look at me."

"Me deaf—you blind. What a couple of brave souls."

Their laughter clatters against the walls, bouncing away from the stage and then back at them again.

"Still," Cass says. "I wonder sometimes what it'll be like when we leave Verona High. When I have to go to a campus where no one's seen me, and every single time I hit the sidewalk, people will be giving me double takes. Or trying to pretend that the thing on my face doesn't matter, which feels as bad as pretending it's not there at all."

"And majoring in—"

Cass takes a deep breath. Shakes her head. "Do you know?"

"I want it to be music. But I couldn't even teach music, not with—" He points at his throat. "I hate that the majors that make the world a beautiful place never do seem to translate into money. It's horrible jobs that pay real salaries. You know—like data entry or teeth pulling."

Again, laughter.

"We never would have gotten to know each other without this place," Dylan says softly. "Maybe that's why this happened—so we'd forget ourselves long enough to finally meet. I feel like that—like I've been so consumed with what everyone thinks about me that I've never actually met most people."

"Life would be better if it were a musical," Cass insists. "You could sing yourself through the whole thing. Get good grades on your finals, and you could tap dance down the hall-way. Get your finger slammed in a locker door, and you could belt out something really sad—sadder than a funeral dirge. It'd be nice to have applause now and then."

"What about when the guy gets the girl?" Dylan asks. "What's that sound like?"

When Cass doesn't answer right off, he holds out his hand. "Maybe we should go find out."

They sit at the piano together; Dylan strikes a few chords, and Cass strings together a new melody line. They're impro-vising, just as they improvised on the first day when Cass joined in on Dylan's music from the Avery's front step.

Without a stutter, Dylan sings, too; their harmony is emo-tional, rhythmic. I start to sway.

Until my phone vibrates.

twenty-four

The ring tone's off, allowing for an enormous sigh of relief to mingle with the dust particles floating around my head. But I tense up again, wondering *Who could possibly need me?* as I scramble after the phone. When I check to see who's called, I find that its screen has come alive and a new black-and-white scene is playing.

I'm staring at the Avery of old. "OPENING NIGHT" is blazing across its marquee. It appears everyone in town is arriving—a bunch of round-fendered cars are fighting for parking spaces. Men in their finest pressed suits and women in gorgeous new hats are filing down the front walk, toward the entrance.

Once inside, they find their seats; the entire theater buzzes with excitement as the orchestra tunes up.

The lights fall.

I can see him in the pit. Nick. He raises his hands, places them on the keys.

This is it.

I hold my breath. And keep holding.

Emma misses her cue. She isn't standing on the deck of the ship, beneath the stoplight. In fact, she isn't on the stage at all.

"Come on," Nick whispers, as though hoping he can make her instantly appear. "Come on."

She bursts out, her feet clomping awkwardly across the deck. And pauses. The introductory measures of "All Through the Night" hit the air and die. The only part of her that moves is her mouth, but nothing's coming out. She licks her lips repeatedly, in a way that says her mouth is as dry as clothes left out on the line in a windstorm.

Now what?

Her breath quickens as she stares out into the darkened theater. The introductory measures of her song hit the air a second time. The music falters as she stands frozen, her mouth clamped shut. The first line continues to elude her.

Nervous rustling ripples up from the crowd—chairs squeaking. A cough.

She cringes as though the spotlight has begun to burn.

Emma—the valedictorian, successful at everything she's ever put her mind to—is screwing up. As she's never screwed up anything in her life. Whispers filter from the crowd, followed by a satisfied snicker. It sounds as though someone in the audience is announcing, *Finally, finally, here's something she can't do. Little Miss Valedictorian—how smart does she feel now?*

"Don't let them get to you," Nick murmurs. "Just keep moving. Keep moving, keep moving."

From the pit, a few piano notes. The introductory measures of her song. The notes twist, bending into a strangely off, almost minor-sounding chord. A mistake, it seems at first. Only, that minor sound begins to bend, beneath the addition of other notes, into another chord.

Nick's reminding her, "I've got you. . . ."

Emma squares her shoulders, juts her head forward. She nods—she's heard him.

She releases a few notes of her own, a few lyrics. The entire orchestra kicks in—but the piano sings out over all the rest of the instruments. His piano—Nick—is carrying her.

Nick leans into the small light poised on top of the piano, allowing Emma to see him. Emma's voice grows louder beneath his support. He presses the keys more forcefully, pushing her to belt her lyrics. *You can do this,* his chords insist. She believes him; the strength that was missing when she first appeared onstage washes across her face.

The scene on my phone fades to black, then comes back to life again. Now I'm staring at the front of the Avery. The square is quiet. Summer fireflies pop on the green space near the front walk, dance over the pavement, bounce between cars toward the alley. And my screen is following them.

The back door of the theater bursts open. Emma lurches into the moonlit alley, struggling to catch her breath. Nick follows close behind.

I can still hear the applause. It's pouring out the open door. And Emma is laughing. "We did it." She sighs with relief.

Nick pushes the wisps of her hair back from her face and wraps her in his arms.

Surprise washes across her face. Emma's no longer staring at a magazine imagining what it must feel like to be held by a man; she's actually *in a man's arms*. Nick smiles broadly, relishing the trusting weight of Emma's body pressing against him.

Nick's face lowers slowly. As their lips meet, a soft glow begins to emanate from the space around their heads.

This is no mere spark, as I saw snap between them when they met. This is no mere soft glow on the distant horizon. As their kiss lingers, the entire sky above warms to a yellow-green hue. The stars grow closer, joining together above them.

There's something magical about this kiss. It's no shy first kiss, not like the awful thing I shared with Matt Fredericks during the seventh-grade field trip. It's the kiss that brightens the sky and shifts the night wind, blowing discarded candy wrappers and programs underfoot.

"Emma!" George's muffled voice shouts from somewhere deep inside the Avery. "Where are you?"

Nick pulls his mouth away. Yellow-green swirls instantly fade from the night sky.

A single tear trails down Emma's cheek.

"What is it?" Nick asks. "What's the matter?"

"It feels like everything's already been plotted out for us. In two more weeks, the play closes. You'll pack up your sheet music, step away from the Avery's orchestra, and head to the train depot. By the end of the summer, I'll be gone, too. Gone to college out east."

"But Emma—"

"It doesn't even feel like real life, somehow. You and me. It feels like a break from real life. Like—intermission. A little space between Act I and Act II, Childhood and Adulthood."

"Maybe not," Nick whispers.

"What else is there? You won't have a job—you'll have to go home. I have to go to school. And the more I think about it, the clearer it all is what'll happen to me at school. I'll be bookish, practical Emma Hastings. I'll go to dances. I'll meet a nice, sensible boy. The kind of boy my father would approve of. Someone studying to become a doctor or lawyer. And after graduation, we'll do the sensible thing. We'll get married. In the beginning, I'll teach. Probably something in the humanities. Maybe Latin." She pauses to chuckle. "Latin. A dead language. And then I'll quit to have children. Two. Maybe three. My days will all be about picking the newspaper off the living-room floor. Tying shoelaces. Measuring out teaspoons of baking soda. I'll host dinner parties, and my husband's coworkers will pat me on the head because they like my Jell-O molds and my martinis. We'll all come back here to visit Dad. Maybe see a show at the Avery now and again. And I'll be dying inside, trying desperately not to remember the time when the Avery felt magical and our love was exciting and how I became a different person on that stage."

"Emma, you're overreacting."

"No. Absolutely not. I know Dad doesn't like you."

Nick frowns. "He doesn't—"

"I didn't say that right. It's not that he doesn't like you. He doesn't like how I feel about you. It scares him. And the idea of what the rest of my life will look like after you're gone scares me."

"Emma! The star needs to take her bow!" George shouts, his pride echoing through the alley.

"I have to go," Emma whispers.

"Emma—our story doesn't have to end this way. I don't want it to end."

But Emma doesn't know what else to say. She wants to stay, but her father—and the real world—is calling to her, tearing her away from Nick.

She pushes past him, through the doorway, back into the Avery.

Above the alley, the stars remain crossed.

The scene fades; my phone's screen is bright white—like a blank page.

I rush to turn off the phone—and realize the handkerchief I found along with the opera glasses is still balled into my fist.

I keep the phone on long enough to open my hand and see, in the glow from the screen, that I'm not holding a handkerchief at all. It's a cloth flower. Under the decades of accumulating dust, it's still sunset pink.

It's Mom's cloth flower—the one she tucked into the sash on her dress to prove she was, in fact, very grown-up.

There's no more music in the theater. No more piano—no more singing.

Cass and Dylan have returned to the stage. Beneath the light filtering across their faces, Dylan takes hold of Cass's hand. He draws her close and they begin to dance.

This is why Cass was so anxious to come. A big part of it, anyway. I can feel it—this is every bit as palpable to me as what had happened between Nick and Emma as they rehearsed.

No—more so. Because we're all right here. This isn't playing out on a screen. It's live. These are the two hearts Bertie predicted.

As if to answer me, to tell me I'm right, the Avery's bronze-colored faces of the theater—hanging on either side of the stage—begin to glow.

Another glow begins to warm my chest—a tiny flame of jealousy has burst to life inside me. My own first kiss was the stuff of experimentation. Of curiosity. I gravitated toward silly Matt Fredericks for the same reason that Emma read *Love Fiction Monthly*. This connection between Cass and Dylan—it's different. It's the kind of thing that once inspired writers to pen the stories inside *Love Fiction Monthly*.

As Dylan strokes Cass's cheek, the spotlight flicks off. But their feet don't scatter. Probably, I think, they don't even know the light is off. Their eyes were already closed.

But the Avery is telling me this scene is not for my eyes to see. It belongs to Cass and Dylan.

So I drop Mom's cloth flower into my backpack. And I slip down the balcony stairs.

twenty-five

A *man needs his secrets.* The phrase sticks in my head like the hook of a catchy pop song. That's what Dylan said, back at the beginning: *A man needs his secrets.*

At this point, my entire life feels like a jumbled mass of secrets—every bit as thick and clumped together as the Avery's cobwebs. Watching Cass and Dylan in the Avery is my secret. The two of them sneaking off to be together in the theater is theirs. The ever-changing production is a secret the entirety of Advanced Drama keeps from Ms. Drewery.

Magic is both the most closely guarded secret of all and as out in the open as Mom's check sheet when Cass and Dylan work together during rehearsal. Cass recites her lines and performs each song with a power that makes every eye in the room glitter; invariably, she sneaks glances at Dylan, her eyes asking him for signs that he approves. His accompaniment is so spot-on that no one—not even Kiki—suggests adding other instruments. Instead, we put two wide-frequency microphones on the soundboard, one on each end. He's all we need.

We lean on him, the same way that Emma leaned on Nick. I can tell from the way Dylan squares his shoulders, the way that his notes thunder, that he's aware of it. That being depended on feels every bit as good to him as it did to that awkward, out-of-town piano player decades ago.

The air changes when Cass and Dylan are front and center. It buzzes; it's electric, it hums like the neon sign on the front of the Avery.

And it powers my pen. Cass and Dylan can't wait to get back into the theater—and neither can I. I use every opportunity, any excuse I can come up with to get out of the apartment, tiptoe up to the balcony, and write, erase, rewrite, keep scribbling in the back of Bertie's journal—new scenes, new ideas all competing for space. Not that they need to. New blank pages keep appearing, one right after another, every time I come to the end of one.

The past and present surround me. When I'm in the Avery, I can let my imagination fly—I describe Cass and Dylan dancing on the stage, and I picture Nick and Emma joining them, their laughter adding new melodies to dance to. Bertie sitting beside me, applauding.

I'm careful, though—every bit as cautious with Cass and Dylan as I am with Mom. I make sure that Dylan, who is always the first of the two to arrive, never sees me in the balcony. And I always make sure that I'm already safely across the street should Cass stop by Potions on her way home.

My mind is bursting with thoughts, sometimes coming faster than I can write.

Thoughts I can't wait to get back to rehearsal and share.

On a Saturday morning just days before opening, I wake up to a tongue. And a wet nose.

I crack an eye, but my eyes are useless without my glasses. All I can see is a gray blob.

But I have a theory.

"Jerry Orbach, that better be you," I mutter, reaching for my glasses on my nightstand. Cat's-eye glasses to see a dog. There's irony for you.

Jerry Orbach climbs into my bed, stretches out beside me.

"Your mom let us in on her way out," Cass says, digging through my closet. "She called me early this morning. I promised her we'd help."

"Promised her what, exactly? Why are you promising her things that I don't know about? Why wouldn't Mom tell me?" Nothing makes sense. Maybe because I have Saturday brain. Maybe because I have dog slobber all over my face. Or maybe, just maybe, none of this actually does make sense.

"Look, she's worried about the show," Cass says. "Apparently, we sold a bunch of tickets in the beginning, but sales have slowed to a crawl since. I promised we'd help out. You know—with the promos. Print ads are apparently not cutting it anymore. We have an interview." She's wearing what would be a decidedly normal outfit—black slacks and a black-and-white-striped blouse—if it wasn't for the yellow plastic platform shoes. When she catches me looking, she shrugs. "I gotta be me."

"Wait. An interview? I don't know anything about interviews."

"She thought you'd say that. She thought I'd do a better job of getting you to the station."

Jerry Orbach moans as I pull my legs out from under the blankets. "Where's Mom, anyway?"

"She had some stuff to do. We're getting close, you know."

"Yeah. I'm aware."

"I mean to opening night."

"Right. I was following."

"Quin, don't you have anything in your closet with any personality at all?"

"I might be able to help you pick something out if I knew exactly where we were going."

Cass finally pulls out a simple white blouse and a pair of dark jeans. "My favorite radio station," she announces. "Hurry up. We've got to get Jerry Orbach back home—and we're picking Dylan up on the way."

We drop off Jerry, then hit the Michaelses' house, which is neither as tiny as my own apartment nor as sprawling as Cass's house. It's average, in the same way I suppose Dylan is always wishing that *he* could be average. He emerges through the front doorway in khakis and a button-down shirt.

I start to get into the backseat, but Cass shoots me a *what's up with you?* frown. I realize I'm a hair from giving my eaves-dropping away—the only reason I'd ever let Dylan have my seat is because I knew, based on what I'd seen at the Avery, that things were changing between him and Cass. So I pretend I was only shifting my weight.

The radio station's a hole in the wall in a small shopping center off the highway. The inside has room for a couple of desks facing a bunch of dials and gauges. On one of the desks, a computer monitor's screen saver displays the station logo.

And both desks hold microphones. It's the microphones that draw Cass's and Dylan's attention.

The DJ's mostly bald, with a rim of white hair around the edge of his head. He waves us in. But Cass and Dylan have turned to statues. I have to push them forward.

"So!" he shouts, gesturing toward the chairs on the opposite side of the desk, each of which has its own small microphone attached to a short stand.

I glance over my shoulder. Dylan has already relegated him-self to the back corner, his chin tucked down toward his chest.

I sit. Reluctantly, Cass takes a spot beside me.

"You're Cass's favorite station," I try, nudging her. But she only offers a slight nod. She's pale and her eyes are wide and she's chewing on the inside of her cheek—something I haven't seen her do since the always-horrifying prospect of changing clothes in middle school gym. It hits me: She thought this would be my interview. That her job was getting me to the station. That she and Dylan were just my moral support.

"Ms. Drewery already told me all about you," the DJ assures us. "No need for a bunch of fussy introductions. I'm going to ask a few quick questions. We'll do it live, but with your permission, I'd like to record it, too. So I can replay it several times between now and the day of the show. Help you continue to sell tickets."

"That's—great." Now it's my turn to gnaw on my cheek. If that's any indication of how I'm going to answer his questions on air, this is going to be the worst interview of all time. "I wish Mom was here," I mutter, hoping it's too soft for anyone to hear.

The DJ smiles, trying to calm our nerves. "Ms. Drewery was my teacher. She always did love that theater. It'll be a delight to help out."

And with the flick of a few switches, a light indicates we're live.

Cass flinches. And swivels in her chair, turning her birthmark away from the DJ. I can hear what she said back in the Avery—about how it hurts when people pretend her birthmark doesn't exist. I wonder, with an awful sick feeling, if my forgetting about her birthmark over the years has hurt her, too. But I have no idea how to not call attention to it and not pretend it isn't there, all at the same time. Right now, I have no idea how to rescue her. How to be her friend. And it terrifies me.

"We're joined today by the director and two cast members of the Verona High production of *Anything Goes*," he declares, his voice low and smooth, like velvet.

We nod.

My face burns. We're nodding. On the radio.

"Yes," I blurt, leaning so close to the microphone that a nearby speaker wails.

The DJ motions for me to lean back from the mic.

"Actually," I manage, "Dylan and Cass are both involved in the music. Cass is the lead—Hope Harcourt. The star of the show. And Dylan's the musical director."

"Well! We certainly need to hear from him. Why don't you give us a few words—"

No no no. Me and my big stupid mouth.

I look over my shoulder. Just as I feared, Dylan's got that whole wrongly-arrested-and-shackled-to-an-interrogation-desk look.

"It's going to be powerful," I announce for him. "In fact, Dylan's piano is so strong, it's the only instrument we need. I mean—you know—it's more than just a piano. Because. Dylan's. You know."

"Playing it?" Cass says.

"Right."

"Uh-huh." The DJ's looking at me as though I've blown my nose and laid the damp Kleenex on his desk, right in front of him. He clears his throat. "Well. Since our listeners are fans of musical theater, why not give us a taste."

"Taste?" I croak.

"Sure. Hope, how about a little tidbit to whet our appetites for the show. Why don't you do a few bars of the title song?"

Cass's mouth drops. She clears her throat. Licks her lips— but her mouth is so dry it clicks. "In—" she starts. Coughs. "In—olden . . ."

She flashes me a look of utter, pure horror. She's off. Just like she was on day one. Out of tune. She glances behind her. All Dylan can do is open his hands, flash his palms. Helpless.

I can't let this go on any longer.

"You know," I jump in, "it's a little hard to perform off the cuff, because we're doing a—well, a modern version of the play. Updated," I say, not caring at that moment how close I'm coming to admitting we've rewritten giant chunks of the musical. All that matters is helping Cass. I attempt to flash her a comforting smile. "It's something you have to come see for yourselves."

But I can tell my comfort is cold.

"Yes," the DJ says, clearing his throat. "That's *Anything Goes* at the Verona High auditorium. . . ." As though this interview will ever make anyone want to come see the show now.

Cass covers her port-wine stain with her hand. The door *whoosh*es as Dylan steps outside, waiting for us on the sidewalk.

twenty-six

I'm worried.

Actually, that doesn't quite begin to cover it. Saying I'm worried about the production is like saying you're mildly concerned about finding yourself tied up in the trunk of your kidnapper's car. This is a level of worry I've never reached before. It's a level of worry I would never have believed, just a couple of months ago, was even possible.

Our pathetic attempt at an interview has shaken me.

But it's shaken Cass and Dylan even more. Reality hit them both back in that radio station—hard enough to erase what they've seen in the Avery. They no longer trust that they'll be stars, not in the Verona High auditorium. Instead, they believe they'll be as they were in the station, stumbling in front of microphones and an actual audience. They're quiet during our next few rehearsals. They stare at their sneakers. They don't so much as look at each other.

Everyone else is frantically busy at this point—so into their own jobs, I can't get everyone together at one time so we can run through the whole musical. The class is acting like an entire room of those tiny little rubber balls, all of them bouncing in their own direction. I'm racing around, trying to gather them up. Only I can't hold them all at once. The balls slip out of my grip, and there they go, bouncing crazily.

Every day, someone has a new problem. Liz threatens to come unglued because I didn't mention her idea for the audience to show up in vintage clothing during the interview. The stage crew complains they don't have time enough between scenes to change sets—especially since the "stage crew" also consists of cast members who need to change costumes between sets, too. I'm pummeled with questions about lines. "Really," Kiki says, after reading through an entire page of material. "Does that sound realistic to you?" At which point, I'm suddenly rewriting all over again, until she nods, satisfied that she can pull it off. I'm telling—begging is a better word, actually—Michael (of the red ball caps) to write his own "impossible to memorize" lines on his wrist if he needs to.

And Toby's hauling me to the back of the stage to take a look at his "night sky" screen.

Oh, the screen. He drags me over to look at the thing every day. And it still doesn't work. Not like Toby thought it would—and not like I imagined. I wish he'd scrap the whole idea. Even knowing what it's supposed to be, I don't think "stars" when I see it. I think "old weather-beaten white Christmas lights on a big black sheet."

Still, though, this project isn't mine alone. It's ours—or it's supposed to be. Advanced Drama, senior project. So I nod to every one of his new ideas. "You'll figure it out," I lie.

With every rehearsal, it begins to feel a little less like "ours." It's more like "fragmented." Especially since two of us—Cass and Dylan—just keep retreating, moving farther away from the group. Especially since everyone just keeps bouncing around in increasingly crazier ways.

And every afternoon in the auditorium it happens exactly the same way: right when I start to think I've got all the individual questions answered, every potential meltdown averted, and I'm waving my arms, starting to announce it's time for the whole class to run though the opening scene or that one problematic number, one more time, all together, everyone starts to leave. They're heading out the auditorium door, because they have tests to study for and jobs to get to.

Without fail. Every single time.

And sure, I'm the director—but who am I to say they can't study? Or keep them so long they wind up getting fired?

So they go.

Every time I kill the auditorium lights, officially marking

the end of another rehearsal, I wish worry had a kill switch, too.

Only it doesn't. My worry keeps ballooning, putting a roadblock between me and—well, just about anything: being able to enjoy the unread paperbacks stacked beside my bed, getting hungry enough to actually want food, sleep.

I'm in the midst of yet another night of staring at the dots that make up the numbers on my bedside digital clock when a warm yellow light flickers. It seems to be coming from the square. I grab my glasses and rush to the window. I crack it, only to find it's turned chilly outside, almost uncomfortably so. I shiver against the night air filtering in through the screen.

Across the square, at the Avery, I catch the flicker again. The full moon is dancing across a second-story window. The breath catches in the back of my throat. When has the moon ever flickered?

I clean my glasses for a second look. The light's not moon-light at all—it's coming from the inside. And a man's solid black silhouette fills the window.

George. Mom said she used to see him up there. In the years after Emma died.

What if he's still there?

Not possible. Then again, considering everything else I've seen, why couldn't it happen? Why couldn't George be up there in that apartment? Why couldn't he be standing in the window trying to get my attention?

I jump up, slam my feet into sneakers, and snatch my backpack—it's got everything: my phone, my flashlight, the file and wire clothes hanger I used weeks ago to pop the theater's skeleton key lock. I leave the apartment quietly, then sprint across the square.

I've never been inside the lobby before, only the house where the seats are—but the minute I burst inside, it smells ancient and forgotten. I bounce my flashlight against wallpaper that dangles in strips, like skin peeling after a sunburn. My scalp tightens, and I erupt in a full-body rash of goose bumps.

I should go home.

This place isn't mine to go poking around in. Sure, I've crawled across the balcony, the stage. But those seem like public spaces to me. Now, here I am, trying to get into a space that's decidedly private: George's home. *It's not right to be in there,* I scold myself. Especially alone. In the dark.

And still, I can't make myself head back to the door.

I hurry past the lobby toward a large doorway. But this leads straight to the sea of audience seats. There has to be another door I've never seen. Some way to get upstairs.

I creep down the center aisle. Climb onto the stage, work my way backstage through the dark labyrinth of dressing rooms. And finally find a narrow hall. I stare down it the longest time, like I'm trying to work up the courage to make a leap off a rocky ledge, straight into a shallow pool below.

Finally, my feet start moving. At the end of the long corridor, I find a small door marked Private.

I jiggle the knob.

It gives, exposing a narrow staircase.

I climb, jumping at every squeak and groan—even those created by my own footsteps.

At the top of the stairs, I step into an apartment that seems eerily frozen in time. I call out tentatively, in little more than a whisper—but there's no answer, no evidence that George (or any living creature, for that matter) has been here for years. Living-room furniture is arranged around a large wooden TV cabinet. I stare at the gray screen, imagining it offered George his only link to the outside world after his daughter's death. His rocking chair, wooden arms discolored from his handprints, sits near a fireplace filled with scorched logs and ashes. A circular braided rug covers the floor, and pictures of a girl in various stages of growing up complete the picture of a lived-in home.

I wander into the kitchen, still pointing my flashlight. Dishes line the cupboard; tarnished silverware fills a drawer. A calendar above the small table reads 1957. The coffee percolator remains on the counter. I avoid the fridge, the pantry, fearing food has rotted and decayed there.

I move back through the living room, toward the two bedrooms. Emma's has been frozen in time even longer than the rest of the apartment—since 1947. A light sweater is draped over the back of the chair before her study desk. Pens lean against the inside of a cup beneath a student lamp with a green glass shade. Her bedroom contains few girly frills: no lace-trimmed bedspread, no dressing table littered with tubes of lipstick and bottles of perfume. No hand mirror. No jewelry. Tomorrow's clothes—a blue skirt and a white embroidered blouse—are laid out neatly across her plain yellow bedspread. Clothes that Emma never put on.

George's room is part office, part bedroom. His clothes are neatly spaced in a tiny closet; his pocket watch and chain lie on the dresser, covered in a skin of dust. A large rolltop desk is cluttered with files and stacks of paper—the only area of the entire apartment that seems unorganized.

Boxes of paperwork make a fence around the desk—I stop for a moment to lay down my flashlight and pick through the closest container. The cardboard box, wilted by time and humidity, is itself unorganized, stuffed tight with bills and receipts, as well as drawings from Emma's childhood, programs from theatrical performances, playbills, lobby cards for movies, pictures of Emma, Emma's high school term papers. Even a few news clippings—the same articles Mom kept safe in her hatbox. A smaller folder contains copies of Emma's death certificate and George's marriage license to Emma's mother. I stare at the marriage license an especially long time. Emma's mother's name was Avery.

I find myself getting so interested in the more personal

items—family photos, the hand-drawn birthday cards Emma made George—that I sit in his chair and begin to pile the looked-at items in my lap. Once the stack starts to feel heavy and unwieldy against my legs, I lean forward to put it back into the box—but stop when I notice a large envelope with old-fashioned, slanting cursive writing. "Trouble," it reads.

My fingers barely touch the flap on the back of the envelope when voices begin to tickle my ears.

I slip the unopened envelope into my backpack and hoist the strap over my shoulder. I turn off my flashlight but keep it in my hand.

My raspy breath echoes through the hallway as I slowly inch back toward the living room. The voices grow louder the closer I get.

Relief ripples through me; the voices are pouring from the old black-and-white TV. Fear returns, though, when I wonder, *Who turned it on?*

"Hello?" I croak. "Hello? Mr. Hastings? George?"

But the living room is eerily vacant. The TV flashes images of life as it once was in the apartment. There they are, at the end of the day: Emma with a book in her lap, George twirling the end of his mustache and laughing at his favorite radio show.

The TV's plagued by interference. The image on the screen begins to flip, then turns to black-and-white snow. A crunchy static fills the air, for only a moment, to be replaced by close-ups of wrinkled, furious faces. George shouts, "I forbid it! No more Nick!" while Emma slams her bedroom door. Through the walls, they continue to scream angrily at each other, their voices as tangled as the wild vines that grow up the theater's bricks.

More black-and-white snow; more static.

The screen fills this time with peaceful images. Emma flashes a mannequin-fake smile; she's pretending she's given up. She kisses George's cheek. Once he's asleep, she sneaks out of the apartment, heading downstairs. Nick is waiting for her on the stage in the theater below.

The TV goes black, but the footsteps still echo. They're coming from the stairs now, growing fainter and farther away.

"Emma?" I whisper.

I hurry out of the apartment. "Emma?" I try again, my whisper echoing against the staircase.

Silence.

I race down the stairs, through the backstage area.

I'm back in the lobby. Alone.

Until voices spill from the auditorium.

Cass and Dylan are here.

twenty-seven

"What are we going to do?" Dylan asks.

He's center stage, sitting cross-legged, his shoulders slumped forward. And Cass is pacing. The theater is midnight dark—the only light in the entire room comes from a spotlight that's popped to life, shining down from the ancient rigging. It creates a white circle of light on the wooden stage.

"I don't know," Cass says. She's walking in a circle over and over, tracing the outline of the spotlight. "Everything would be different if we could do our musical in here."

Dylan brings himself to his feet and reaches for her.

It was intended to be a brief moment of comfort—an *it's okay; we'll get through it*.

But the instant his hand touches her arm, it becomes far

more. They don't so much embrace as curl into each other. Cass tucks her head beneath Dylan's chin, resting her smooth, peach-colored cheek against the base of his perfect throat. Each time their skin touches, a tiny burst of sparks flies into the air.

This has never happened before. Dancing—yes. Hand-holding—yes. Creating music together—yes. But not this. Not wrapping their arms around each other, pressing themselves against each other so tightly that they appear more like two strokes of a pen—two curlicues making up the same cursive letter—than they do two different people. They wrap their arms tighter around each other, finally admitting that this has been the stuff of fantasy for both of them.

There's no interest in rushing the moment. They linger—Dylan puts his hand gently on the top of Cass's head, starts to bury his nose in her hair.

But Cass tilts her head back. She catches his eye.

I can feel it—the not-enough of it all. Even though they're the kind of close that means they can feel the warmth radiating from each other's lips.

As Dylan starts to lower his mouth—and I think, with a gasp, *Cass's first kiss*—the entire theater explodes in blinding Technicolor. There is no darkness, only brilliant gilding and vivid red curtains. Instantly, the entire set is new again. Staircases stand tall. The smell of sawdust and paint fills the air, dancing alongside the electric sensation that a show is about to begin.

But a strange ticking fills my ears—an annoying, persistent countdown clock insists Cass and Dylan can't stay in the theater forever, just as Emma and Nick couldn't. These fleeting moments together under the lights are an intermission from the real world. In the real world, which comes with a strict set of guidelines and rules and restrictions, "limitless" is more of a metaphor than a word used literally.

No—here, during intermission, there are no limits. The truly impossible can take place. Here, during intermission, Cass and Dylan loom far larger than their physical bodies would have ever allowed. In here, they are CinemaScope. A symphony swells out of nowhere, playing a sweeping love overture. A summer breeze trickles across my face, carrying the smell of wildflowers that bloomed more than a half century ago, for Emma and Nick. Fireflies flash through the darkness. Stars blink across the ceiling, forming an X.

And because anything is possible, even the persistent ticking no longer sounds like a clock, but like the running of an old-fashioned projector.

Stars begin to slide away from each other. Bertie predicted this. Cass and Dylan—mirror images of Emma and Nick—have taken up where the couple from the past left off. They're the ones who are responsible for moving those stars—uncrossing them. Righting the tragedy of Emma and Nick. *This is it. . . .*

I hold my breath as Dylan's mouth hovers over Cass's. I feel I'm intruding, but I can't take my eyes off the stage. I lean forward, in anticipation of an utter explosion of magic—like nothing any of us has seen yet.

Instead, the door to the alley flies open with a bang. Cass and Dylan gasp, pulling away from each other. Fireflies stop dancing; the smell of wildflowers is replaced with the smell of dust and mildew. The stage returns to its shabby self.

Above, the stars slide back into a giant X.

"Wh-wh-wh—?" Dylan stutters.

Cass's face shines in the spotlight; her birthmark is back. Her hand flies to her face. She knows it's back.

I slip down behind a row of seats. Has someone reported us for trespassing?

The stars fade. The spotlight dies.

"Hello?" a voice cries out. "Hello?"

I should know that voice. Moonlight spills from the alley into the dark theater, illuminating the small silhouette.

George? No—not George. The voice is female.

"I know you're in here. I've been watching."

It's Kiki. And she's ruining everything.

I close my eyes, hoping that when I open them again, Kiki will be gone, and Cass and Dylan will be able to recapture the magic. I hear Mom's bedtime-story voice: "They were torn apart, Romeo and Juliet, by outside forces—their families didn't want them to be together. Just like George was afraid that Emma would run off with Nick! He pulled them apart, too! Yes! It's all the same, don't you see?"

But when I open my eyes, nothing's changed. The theater's dark and silent and scary. No Technicolor. No CinemaScope. It's happened with Cass and Dylan, too—the outside world has encroached. And Kiki's the one who's let that outside world in. She's letting it tear two hearts apart.

"Hello?" Kiki tries again. This time, even from a distance, I can tell she's trembling. She's uninvited and unwanted.

Cass and Dylan stand quietly—close to each other, but no longer together. They back up. They're hurrying away from the stage in opposite directions.

"Don't think I can't hear you running around in here," Kiki shouts, her voice echoing. "Hello? I know you're in here. Cass! Dylan!

"Hello?" she cries out again, crossing her arms over her chest protectively.

She tries to take a step forward but waves her hands in front of her face, lets out a bunch of spurts. In the moonlight streaming from the still-open alley door, I can see that a wall of cobwebs has lowered, forming a barrier.

She takes a step to the side, moving completely out of the moonlight.

I can't see her, but I can hear her shuffling.

Around me, though, the Avery groans and creaks back at her, in complete dissatisfaction. Groans like the old, arthritic woman she is, angry that her home has been disrupted, intruded upon. The smells of dust and rot and wet decay explode.

A scurry of small feet across the floor and a squeak are followed closely by Kiki's horrified shriek. I've never encountered any kind of rodent inside the theater—never seen so much as an ant—but a rat apparently just skittered across Kiki's feet.

I hear a deep, throaty inhale. Feel a waft of muggy air across my face. The Avery is sighing in annoyance, telling Kiki, *Give it up. I'm not letting you in. You're not welcome. You're not the right heart. And you are not here for the right reason.*

As punctuation, a board slips from the ceiling and clatters to the floor. Kiki's trespassing—Cass and Dylan are the welcome ones. The Avery is letting Kiki know it.

After another threatening groan from the theater, Kiki lets out a final yelp and lunges through the back door, into the alley.

I pull myself to my feet and drag myself down the center aisle. After Kiki's intrusion, the theater smells old. It smells like disappointment. It smells like the real world.

Cass and Dylan are nowhere in sight by the time the alley door shuts behind me. As I cross the square, heading for home, I look back over my shoulder.

The Avery remains dark, its corners concealed by over-grown, half-dead vines and shrubs. Windows are cracked. Bricks are still spray-painted STAY OUT! and No Trespassing!! All of it hiding the magic I know is still locked inside. Protected from uninvited meddlers.

twenty-eight

We have one more shot at getting this thing right. Dress
rehearsal.

Cass and Dylan are every bit as closemouthed about
what happened the night before as the Avery itself was sitting
quietly under the moon. They don't look at each other. They
don't speak to each other. Cass barely even speaks to me.

Toby's hung his screen at the back of the stage. When
he turns it on, the lights in the center twinkle. But the lights
along the top let out a buzz and die. And as he and I stand
in the middle of the stage staring, the top corner pulls loose
from the rigging he's attached it to. It plummets like a bird
that's been shot, then swings over to the left side of the stage,
dangling pitifully.

"Just keep going," I order, consulting Bertie's journal—it

is, after all, filled with every new scene I've written. I clap my hands in rhythm, hoping to get them all riled up—the same way fans stomp the bleachers to cheer their team to glory.

I say it a lot, actually: "Just keep going!" when someone misses a cue. "Just keep going!" when Dylan's music falls from the stand. "Just keep going!" when he tries to start playing again but is so flustered, he only winds up striking a bunch of sour notes. "Just keep going!" when two of our actors bump into each other so hard, they knock each other flat on their rears. "Just keep going!" when Kiki breaks the fourth wall—that invisible dividing line between the audience and the stage—as she stomps right past the footlights to tell me, "This line still sounds awful."

"Just—just!" I shout when one of the girls cries out backstage that she can't find her costume and another actress steps forward, shrugging, pointing at her own outfit and saying, "I guess that's why this didn't fit right."

"Just!" I shout when one of the red ball caps gets so frustrated, he starts doing a made-up dance routine in the middle of the stage.

"Just!" I shout when another is so lost in all my adding and deleting of scenes that he starts reciting lines he's memorized from *Return of the Jedi*.

But at a certain point, somewhere in the middle of Act II, each "Just keep going" turns into "Please." As in, "Please pretend that chair was supposed to fall." "Please don't point at a skirt that's on backward and start laughing." "Please don't do battle with invisible swords out of nowhere. If you have to improvise, please do something in keeping with the scene."

On that last "please," I look up and find Mom standing beside me, her arms folded across her chest.

The longer I stare, the more I become aware that my eyes are pleading now. Begging her to step in. I'm asking her, with all her years of experience teaching drama classes as talentless as ours, to save this ridiculously bad production.

But all she does is drape an arm around my shoulder and ask for everyone's attention, then adds preposterous encouragement. "Never fear. A bad dress rehearsal only means you'll have a great first performance."

"You can't be serious," I mutter.

Up on the stage, Toby is taking down his screen. "I got this, Quin. I'm taking it home, and it will be perfect for opening night."

"I repeat: you cannot be serious."

"Completely," Mom insists. "The worse the dress rehearsal, the better the opening night. I think it focuses everyone's attention."

"Then judging by this mess, we should all be up for Tonys this year."

Mom laughs, starts backing up. She's talking and leaving at the same time, giving me no chance to argue with her. "I'm so positive, I took out a full-page ad in the paper for tomorrow.

'Anything Goes in the Verona High auditorium!' I have no wor-
ries." She's either completely flipped or has suddenly become
Meryl Streep. "Take Cass somewhere after she changes. The
two of you go do something fun to clear your heads."

Only we don't. I drop her off at her house because she
needs to feed Jerry Orbach. At least, that's what she says. But
Jerry is quickly becoming her go-to *gotta wash my hair* excuse.

It's not that she's avoiding me, though. It's the Avery she's
got on her mind. I'm sure of it. So much so, I putter around
inside Potions. I even hang the Open sign in the door. Not
that I care about making any sales. I'm just staying in the
store to keep an eye on the front of the old theater. To see the
moment Cass decides to show up.

Until the bell jingles, announcing the arrival of an actual
customer. At least, I assume it's a customer. Until I turn
toward the door.

"Aren't you going?" Kiki grumbles.

"Going?"

She rolls her eyes. "To the theater."

When I don't answer, she runs her fingers through her
frizzy orange hair and growls. "Come on, Quin. Admit it. You
were there last night. You and Cass and Dylan. I was there,
too. The alarm got tripped at Ferguson's, and Dad and I drove
down there to check on the place. Nothing. He said it was
probably some stray cat. I figured it was probably some stray
kid on his bike, heading toward the alley behind the Avery. So

I checked. And lo and behold, the back door wasn't shut. And there were voices inside. Some kind of light."

"Kiki, I have no idea—"

"Yes, you do. You know. What're you guys doing in there, anyway? Playing some sort of twisted game of hide-and-seek? I don't know what the draw is. I've never known what the draw is. It's an old, empty building, like the rest of the old, empty buildings on the square. I don't know why your mom's so into the idea of saving it—so something bad happened there. So what? Bad things happen inside buildings all the time. People have heart attacks and keel over. I bet at some point, someone got hit by a train. Why not save that dilapidated old depot? Maybe somebody choked on their dinner in the Fred Harvey restaurant. Why not save that?"

I try to act like I'm too busy stamping prices on perfume bottles to pay any attention to her. I know she never made it all the way in. But I get the distinct feeling that she is aware that she was pushed out. That the Avery evicted her. Kept her from exploring inside. She's working me for more info.

"What's the matter with your mom, anyway?" she goes on. "Is she senile? The rest of the town's humoring her because she was their teacher?"

Now she's got my hackles up. I narrow my eyes.

"You can save us all, you know."

"From what?" I growl.

"From that musical. From total failure."

I glance up at her over the rim of my glasses.

"Seriously. Think about it. You and Cass and Dylan go over there. Just like you have been. Like maybe you guys are even planning to do later today—I don't know. Then I call the police—anonymously. I report somebody trespassing. You guys get picked up. Say you go to Verona High.

"And because you've mentioned the school, they call the principal. And even at Verona High, where nobody ever gets in trouble, not really, where we all are expected to commit our fair share of adolescent shenanigans, the principal has to show the town that he's in charge. So you guys get suspended."

"Why would I want to get suspended? Why would I want to get—"

"Because then, with the director and the lead and the musical director unable to perform, the musical is canceled."

"But we're suspended."

"Isn't being suspended better than being humiliated in front of the entire town?"

A flame of anger pops inside of me. "Get out of here, Kiki. I mean it."

"What's there to be mad about? We're terrible. There's no way around it. Maybe Cass and Dylan had a couple of great moments during rehearsal. But so what? Sometimes I can sound half decent singing in the shower. What matters is how you perform when the pressure's on. And I'm telling you, this is going to be the worst performance ever in the history of high school musicals."

"Get out of here," I repeat through gritted teeth. "I'm not getting suspended just to rescue you. You're getting on that stage opening night, and you are going to perform with the rest of us subpar humans. And if you try to call in sick, I'm going to go to your house and drag you to the auditorium.

"I wouldn't push me," I warn. "After all, you just admitted to me that *you* were the one inside the Avery. You were trespassing. Seems I could call you in, report you. Right?"

She flashes me a nasty look, slowly retreats. The bell on the door announces when she's finally gone.

twenty-nine

More than ever, I want to get back to the Avery. All the pieces are here, but they're still in a giant jumble: Cass and Dylan being transformed on the stage, the past playing out scene by scene, the predictions.

The Avery isn't talking to everyone. Not everyone sees the sparks. Not everyone is allowed inside.

Just me—I'm the only one who's seen it all, every last bit, ever since that first day on the square. That's my name on Bertie's journal.

The clock is ticking. Opening night is upon us. The chance to save the Avery—the town. I see some of the connections, sure. But what do I do with it? What's the big picture? This story opened itself up to me—why?

After dark, I sneak out of Potions. I rush to the alley

behind the Avery, ready to attack the back door with my coat hanger key.

But stop abruptly when I find the door is completely rusted shut. And not in the way I found the side door to the theater rusted shut the first night I tried to get inside. This isn't a little skim of rust that's formed along the cracks. Rust covers the entire door, all the way around. So much of it, so thick, it completely conceals the lock—and the hinges—and even the doorknob. It looks like a thick scab that's grown over a deep wound.

Head spinning, I stumble out of the alley to the front door. More rust. So much of it, the padlock and chain around the knob here have no shape at all—they make little more than a slight bulge. But when I touch the rust, it's gritty; it flakes a little.

I dive toward the overgrown bushes at the front of the theater, reaching for one of the large rocks that surround the roots—part of what was once a meticulously landscaped area.

I suck in a breath and frantically begin to beat the bulge on the door. Rust rains, falling in crusty orange bits onto the cracked front step.

I pause and quickly glance about, hoping I haven't given myself away by making so much noise. Hoping that Mom—or, for that matter, Kiki—isn't now rushing my way, trying to figure out what the noise was.

But no one comes—the square is as empty as ever.

A gasp rattles in the back of my throat as I turn toward the door, anxious to find out if I'm any closer to freeing the padlock. Because the rust is regrowing, filling in any dents I've made.

The Avery's keeping me out. Period.

Refusing to give up, I squeeze between a wild, overgrown bush and a window. Cup my hands around my eyes and try to see into the lobby. But it's too dark. All I can see is my own hazy reflection.

Voices tickle the back of my neck. I stop breathing. Has someone come? Did I make too much noise?

But they're not coming to the theater's entrance. They're in the alley.

I creep cautiously toward the back of the building, crane my neck to peer around the corner. Watch Dylan run his hands across the door. "C-can't f-find th-the lock-ck."

"But this has always worked," Cass protests. "Use your skeleton key."

Dylan points at the thick slab of rust. "Wh-where?"

"What if we never get back in?" Cass asks. Her desperate tone reveals that what she's really asking is *What if I never see myself that way again?*

Dylan places his hand flat against the rusty door, pleading for this not to be true.

"Maybe it always had to end." Cass sighs. "I mean, what did I think, that every time we had a play, I could come in here and I would always look—and you would be able—? What makes me think anyone else would even see it? It's like we were always in the middle of a game of dress-up."

I retreat, slipping out of the alley. "The right hearts," I whisper. "The right reasons."

I'm still struggling to put the pieces together when I hear the unmistakable sound of Cass's VW revving to life. They're leaving.

"What are you doing?" I ask the Avery. "I don't understand. Cass and Dylan don't have the right reasons? It's not enough to only want magic for yourself? Is that what you think? That I only want this for me, too? Why are you treating me like Kiki—like an intruder?"

The rust, though—it hits me again how much like a scab it looks.

"You're not hurt, are you?" I ask.

Still, no answer.

"Did I do something wrong? Is it because we left the door open? Because we accidentally let Kiki in?"

And still the Avery sits silently.

I'm being pushed. Shoved by some enormous, invisible hand across the square, toward the apartment. Up to my room. I lie on my bed. Sleep doesn't just find me; it attacks. And it sends me straight into a dream.

thirty

Usually when my dreams start, I'm already in the theater. Already in one of the auditorium seats, hugging my legs, pointing my knees skyward. And the curtains draw open, exposing the screen. This time, the dream starts when I'm standing on the square, staring at the theater. The night air isn't crisp like autumn; it's sweet like a memory of a summer night.

The building in front of me is silent, still marred by broken windows and spray-painted No Trespassing warnings. But the neon Avery sign is blazing. And the marquee proclaims, "Tonight! ANYTHING GOES."

I feel as if I'm being given a private invitation to a special performance. I'm certainly not dressed for the theater—I'm still in the same sweats and T-shirt I put on to go to bed. But there's no way I'm going to turn down this invitation.

The moment my feet hit the front walk, the tattered awning above me heals. The buckled walk smooths. There is no rust on the entrance—no padlock. When the door opens, it's with a burst of relief, like the theater's saying, "There you are. I've been waiting for you forever."

The lobby is empty. Flocked wallpaper clings tightly to the walls. A Coca-Cola clock still ticks.

Behind me, a little girl's voice sings out, "The skies say. The skies say . . ." Dahlia skips through the lobby. As she passes me, she seems so small—she'd hate to hear I've thought of her this way. But there it is, anyway: Dahlia's small, a grace note, a little girl in pigtails with a cloth flower tucked into the sash of her dress. "The skies say. The skies say . . ."

"Shhh!" another voices hisses.

I stop breathing as Emma races forward, seemingly out of nowhere. This is the angry Emma I saw on the TV upstairs. She grabs hold of Dahlia's arm, shakes her slightly. "You'll wake my father," she scolds. "It's late. Why aren't you home? How did you get in here?"

"I didn't—I—"

"*Tell me.* How did you get in here?" She digs her fingers deeper into the soft flesh on Dahlia's arm.

"Oooow," Dahlia whimpers. "What's wrong with you? Why are you so mean lately?"

"I'm not."

"You are. You don't have time for me anymore. You used to let me inside. You'd give me free Junior Mints for lunch, and you'd eat Good & Plentys. And it would be our secret—candy for lunch. Only, you don't have time for secrets with me anymore. It's always Nick, Nick, Nick."

It's true. Emma's bristly. Even the loose blond curls on the sides of her face look coarse, like grinding wheels that could wear down anyone who gets too close.

"You don't understand. You're too—"

"No! Don't say that. Don't say I'm too little," Dahlia whimpers. "I'm not too small. I know things. Things you won't ever know, because you don't look up."

Emma frowns in complete confusion. She's never heard this, I think. Bertie's never told her. Maybe Emma, first female valedictorian of Verona High, was always too wrapped up in her facts and figures to look at Bertie's journal, her map.

"I promised," Dahlia insists. "I promised I would look out for you. There's a spell on you— The skies—"

At this point, Emma's frown disappears and she lets out a deep, throaty laugh. "Oh, Dahlia," she says. "Do you ever do anything but cause trouble?"

"But I'm not!"

"Go home, Dahlia. I'm sure your mother will be up to check on you soon. What will she do when she goes to your room and you're not there?"

"But—wait! Don't!"

Emma pushes Dahlia out of the lobby, straight through the entrance—the same one I also found unlocked.

"I know why this door was open!" Dahlia insists. "You left it open on purpose. For Nick. See? I'm not so little that I don't understand. I know—"

Without a word, Emma only pushes Dahlia onto the front walk. I stumble outside, right along with her.

The door slams; a click indicates that Emma just locked it.

"I'm not giving up," Dahlia mutters. "Think some stupid door will keep me out? I promised to look after you. I promised Mom I could keep my flower pretty and clean, and it is—I kept that promise. And I promised I would keep an eye on you, too. And you're more important than some silly old flower. Big people keep promises, and I'm big, and I'm going to keep my promise, too. Just watch."

She's talking to herself, but I respond as though she's given me marching orders. I'm ready to watch—in fact, I'm already on her heels as she races to the side of the building and forces a path behind some bushes. "They've forgotten all about this old fire door," she mutters. "But I haven't. . . ."

Her little hand finds a doorknob. We climb the carpeted steps inside, straight to the balcony.

Mesmerized, I take a seat in the front row. Dahlia props her forearms flat on the railing and plops her chin on the hands she's stacked one on top of the other. The Avery looks especially beautiful, with the chandeliers glowing and the gilding shining on the box seats.

I can see them both clearly: Emma in the center of the stage, beneath a spotlight. And Nick off to the side, slipping out of his jacket. He hangs it with the costumes on the rack positioned side stage. And he joins Emma, stepping into the white circle made by the glowing spotlight. Emma looks happier than I've ever seen her. Even from a distance, that much is clear. And all she's doing is standing with a boy on an empty stage.

Nick reaches for Emma's hand as though to lead her in a dance. "We need music," she murmurs. Her voice echoes through the empty theater.

"We have it," Nick insists. "Don't you hear it?"

He draws her close, humming in her ear. Emma laughs, but her laughter dies as they begin to sway, to dance, to pull each other closer—so close, surely Emma feels the vibrations of his song against her own lips.

Dahlia sighs; she's got a dreamy look on her face. She pulls the cloth flower from the sash on her dress, doing a pantomime routine of a boy giving her the flower. She makes a shy motion with her head, tucking her chin down toward her chest before accepting it, bringing it to her nose, and sniffing its sweet perfume.

Watching her play fills me with a burst of happiness.

Nick's soft song floats from the stage below; Dahlia begins to dance in the aisle, now pretending her flower is a boy, holding her, flirting with her.

Emma takes a step backward, dragging Nick with her, toward the staircases that are part of their set—the two staircases leading up to a platform that represents the deck of the ship for *Anything Goes*. It's so late—the night's performance wrapped hours ago, but the air tingles with the excitement and anticipation of a story about to unfold. They sit together, squeezed tight on the narrow bottom step.

Nick pulls off her glasses. And he kisses her.

Emma puts her head on Nick's chest, right over the heart diagnosed as weak. "Doctors don't know anything about hearts," she says as Nick kisses the top of her head.

She raises her face, and their lips meet once more, just as the main house lights in the Avery come on in a blinding, garish thrust.

"*What* is going on in here?" George bellows, his voice reverberating through the theater. "What is the *matter* with you? Why would you ever entertain the thought of chasing after some tramp, some penniless musician? With everything you have going for you?"

Dahlia stands on her tiptoes, leaning over the edge of the balcony. A fight is erupting. A real fight, in the middle of the stage.

"No," George bellows. "No."

Embarrassed to be treated as a child in front of Nick, Emma shouts at her father, "It's none— You don't—"

"I know," George shouts back. "He looks different to you here. That's the magic of the theater. Everything looks different—"

"Clearer," Emma cries. "Don't you think he sees me differently in here, too? That in his eyes, in here, I'm not clumsy, practical, bookish, predictable Emma Hastings? That I can be—"

"—did not raise you to be some musician's wife—"

"*Wife?*"

"Some lowly musician no better than a hobo—"

The shadows in the Avery lengthen—the angry voices grab the darkest spots and tug at them, dragging them, making them bigger. This argument is vicious. It has teeth.

I squeeze the wooden arms of my seat, hold on against the words swirling like wings, whipping against the inside of the theater, smacking my face, threatening to shove me right out of the balcony.

"Did not raise you—"

"I'm not—"

"You will—"

". . . *love!*"

Emma's shout acts like a blow to George's chest, pushing him backward, making him stumble across the stage.

Silence overtakes the theater as George touches his chest. I can hear his heart thump. Dahlia pants in rhythm to the beat. George's pulse has become hers—become mine—become the pulse of the Avery. Dahlia covers her ears, the beat threatening to burst her eardrums.

George stares at the couple at the edge of the spotlight, still seated on the stairs that have been built for the set. Grasping each other as though to protect themselves from his wide, angry eyes.

"Love him," Emma whispers again. With Nick still holding her glasses, she can't see the impact of her words striking her father.

"Love," I whisper, as though it will sound softer coming from me. I want George to hear me up in the balcony, and to believe it. Want him to stop sending his frantic, out-of-control words to crash through the theater.

Instead, the atmosphere only grows tighter, like a fist. Even the drama masks on the sides of the stage look wracked with pain. I expect desperate wails to pour from their open mouths.

The argument continues to swell, all three voices firing shots at one another. Dahlia presses her hands tighter against her ears, trying to block it out.

George lunges for Emma. Nick holds on tighter. A struggle erupts. A battle over Emma, pushing and kicking and crying out.

Emma squirms to get away. Suddenly, she's climbing—a spur-of-the-moment reaction, it seems—up the narrow stairs with no railing. But she doesn't have her glasses. Nick does. She can't tell where the steps are exactly, not in that blurred mess in front of her. Her feet falter. She stumbles.

"Don't, Emma—" Dahlia warns, but Emma doesn't hear her. Nor does Nick or George.

Nick and George are still shouting, still struggling, when Emma begins to climb again. Her arms fly out in front of her body.

"Emma!" I screech. "Watch out!" The angle of her body is all wrong.

But she can't hear me—no one can.

Emma puts her weight down. She screams at the same moment she finds no step beneath her—only open air. She drops to the stage below, crumpling into a terrible-looking heap, her arms and legs motionless.

George howls, fighting to break himself free of Nick's hold. Trying to get away from him and closer to his daughter. "Emma—" he cries.

Nick hasn't seen her fall. He only wants George to go away. Nick grips George tighter. "Stop it," he shouts. "Leave us alone!"

"Move! She fell! She's hurt," George bellows. Nick spins, seeing his Emma in a scattered-looking pile on the stage.

Nick wails—no words, just utter pain, desperation, shock. His Emma, his love, lying motionless.

Nick's feet pound against the stage. He's running—but he's never been good at running. Dahlia's fingers fly to her mouth; she knows how weak he is, of course she does; how could she forget the day at the depot?

He lunges, grabbing Emma's body and trying to lift her.

His heart isn't up to so heavy a task. Even on the opposite side of the theater, I can feel his chest rip apart, splintering. He screeches and tries to ignore the pain, even as his body fails.

George pushes him aside, or Nick collapses—I can't be sure which at first. His side hits the stage, though, and he stops moving completely.

In George's arms, Emma's limp—her head twisted to the side unnaturally—her neck broken.

Two pairs of footsteps echo through the Avery—George's, as he races to call an ambulance, and Dahlia's, as she races out of the balcony, so fast, she doesn't stop to realize that she's dropped her cloth flower.

"Dahlia!" I cry out. I race down the stairs, chasing after her.

She bursts through the side door, holding her ears—this time, I know, fear is ringing inside them like cymbals being frantically beaten.

"Bertie!" She races across the square to grab the hand of the young woman staring up at the sky. She shakes her arm, trying to get her attention. "They're dying! Nick—Emma— on the stage! I promised—her neck. Help!"

Above, the sky is on fire—yellow and green. And the stars are sliding across the sky, forming a giant X.

"The sky, Dahlia. Look. We're too far south to see the aurora borealis, so it can't be that. It's more. It's magic."

"No! Not now. Don't you understand? They're dying. And you're looking at the sky?"

Dahlia screams because she's never in her life seen anything so horrible—even though it happened on the stage, it isn't play-pretend. It's real. She screams because this time, finally, someone is going to listen. They're not going to treat her like silly little Trouble.

She screams until her mother drops her hat in the front window and the waitresses in the corner booth café and the owner of the hardware store come running. But her mother's shaking her finger at her, and the hardware store owner is relieved because he thought *she* was hurt, and it's all moving far too slowly. Nick and Emma will never be saved.

A tear trails down Dahlia's cheek. "It's too late," she begins to mutter.

"No," Bertie insists, pointing to the sky. "They aren't dead. Don't you see? You can't believe an end that isn't really an end. Don't you remember what I told you? The skies talk. They make predictions. The next time pure hearts meet up in the Avery—at the right time . . . You'll see. The next scene will play out. The final act. This sky, Dahlia. It will come to life, and it will change things. Next time . . ."

"Emma is too dead, Bertie." Dahlia's pain brings tears to my own eyes. "I said I'd watch out for her. I didn't save her."

In the background, a distant siren finally begins to wail.

thirty-one

My eyes pop open. Dahlia's little-girl scream is pulsing inside my ears. The dream was different. For the first time in the roughly ten years I've been having it, the details have shifted. I've never seen Nick's and Emma's deaths. I've never heard Mom scream on the square. The scene was alive—*is* alive. I can still feel the intensity of the fight that erupted between Nick, Emma, and George—the desperation that shredded the air inside the Avery.

More than that—I feel like I'm caught in a fight of my own. I feel as though I'm being shaken awake. I kick at the blankets, jumping out of bed as if I've suddenly found it filled with spiders.

The Avery. It comes to me with urgency: *Go look at the Avery.*

I race across my room, sliding on my glasses as I press my face close to the window. The neon sign above the theater is broken, no longer able to send out a yellow "Avery" to glow against the black sky. The marquee is blank—no current production, no starring names. Streetlights on the square—and throughout Verona, for that matter—give the horizon a soft-white glow. But it's too dark to tell if the rust-scab is still stretched over the front door, barring entrance.

The dream feels so close. I wasn't just watching this play out on a screen; I was in the balcony with Dahlia. In the square with Bertie. It wasn't like I had the ability to change anything that happened. No one even knew I was there. But I *was* there—wasn't I? I had to be. I can easily recall the plush, velvety feel of the balcony seat's upholstery. I can smell the lingering scent of butter in the lobby. Usually when I dream of the night in 1947, I see it all in larger brushstrokes. This last dream—it was as though someone drew it in using the tiniest, most intricate pen tip. I saw it all—including the strands of hair that had worked loose from Dahlia's pigtail and the mole under Emma's left ear. How does a mind come up with all that? Or does it? Are dreams ever that elaborate?

What just happened?

I'm waffling back and forth: Do I dismiss the dream as an overactive imagination able to see more clearly because the story is far more real to me now than it ever has been? Do I empathize with Mom—and Emma and Nick—more than ever? Or do I think the Avery had something to do with it? That it's sending me a message?

I'm still staring at the front of the building when a white crack tears forcefully through the sky. It draws a jagged line between the stars, smashing against the earth with an eardrum-shattering boom. My hands fly to my ears, which pop and ring like my head is a cymbal that's been whacked with a mallet.

"What was that?" Mom calls from her bedroom.

She patters into my room, sticks her face against the window. She stares through a separate pane from the one I'm looking through, but our faces are so close, our cheeks nearly brush. Smoke billows from a distant spot on the horizon.

The phone rings; Mom and I both jump. She darts back out of my room to answer. Her voice is agitated. Her conversation short.

I stare, watching the smoke continue to billow.

"Quin!" she shouts. "Hurry. We've got to go. The school's on fire."

We burst out of the house, Mom wearing mismatched flannel pajamas beneath a beige overcoat and chenille slippers. I come out in my sleep sweats and flip-flops. It's too cold for the flip-flops; the moment the chilly night air starts chewing at my toes, I instantly regret them. But there's no way I can ask Mom to wait for me to grab another pair. Not the way she's moving; the car engine roars to life before I've even swung the passenger door open all the way.

My eye is on the Avery—dark and silent in the rearview— as Mom's car lurches out of her parking space. As she backs up, the front of the old theater looms larger. I think I see it, beneath the nearby streetlight: a padlock on the front door.

Is the rust-scab gone? Why? Has it healed? Has it opened itself back up? Why did it lock me out in the first place?

What are you saying? I want to scream at the Avery.

The theater quickly shrinks as Mom's car careens out of the square.

She flips through radio stations until her dial hits a spot offering local news. I recognize the voice—this is her former student, the one who interviewed us at his station. ". . . word that a fire has broken out at Verona High. Verona fire teams are on their way. As soon as there's an update, we'll be breaking into regular programming live. . . ."

Mom swerves into the lot, her tires squealing. At least, I think they squeal. It's hard to tell for sure because sirens are on top of us now. She pulls to the side as a red fire truck passes by, kicking up the kind of gravel-filled burst of wind that makes my eyes sting.

The truck comes to a stop in front of the school, and fire-fighters in enormous yellow suits climb out. Knee-high rubber boots hit dry pavement.

There are no puddles here in the parking lot. Absolutely no sign it rained. But I know I saw a lightning bolt. A giant white crack etching its way through the sky. Followed by thunder. But there was no rain?

The parking lot lights illuminate Verona High. The familiar two-story redbrick building has always seemed to take on different appearances depending on the time of year: In early fall, when summer heat lingers, it looks like a pizza oven. In midwinter, surrounded by two inches of snowfall, it looks like the start of a Norman Rockwell painting. Now, though, under the garish parking lot lights, with headlights from vehicles drawing an ever-moving pattern across the front and with smoke pouring out through the roof, it looks kind of sinister.

I cross my arms over my chest, trying to protect myself against the chill of night. Mom stomps toward a crowd of faculty members, all of them in their pajama bottoms and house shoes.

Other cars are pulling into the lot, too—students and parents arriving, coming to see the show. My classmates are aiming their phones, some of them at the building, some at the shocked faces of the crowd, and others at the sight of the principal in his red-checkered robe and matching pants.

Most of the faces in the crowd are recognizable: the teachers, Vanessa from Duds, Dylan's dad, Cass's mom, the librarian. I pass by most of their faces often enough that they seem like town landmarks. And every one of them stares up at the school with the same mix of disbelief and shock. Because they all once called Verona High their own. After all, nobody moves to Verona as an adult—what would draw them here? You're born in town, and you either move away or you stay and get old. If they've got gray hair, they were born in Verona. Period.

Verona High is part of who they are. It's the gym where they scored the winning game point and the lunchroom where they met their future husband. The hallway where they had their first kiss, in the middle of their first formal dance. The desk they carved their initials into in room 103, English III. The stairwell where they sat to cram, last minute. The water fountain they tampered with to squirt straight into the eyeball of anyone who stopped for a drink.

No matter the sign of aging—graying hair, reading glasses perched on the ends of noses, potbellies hanging over the drawstrings of sleep pants—tonight as they sadly put their fingers over their mouths and shake their heads, memories wash over them, making them all look seventeen again.

Verona High is our story. Mine, and Emma's, and Mom's, and anyone else's who happens to be standing in that parking lot.

And it bothers me—a lot, actually—that our combined stories might very well be going up in flames inside the school.

I watch the action playing out around me. My eyes settle on the firefighters barking into walkie-talkies, then on the hoses, which they've tugged free from the truck and which now lie flat on the parking lot. No water.

Why aren't they aiming giant, forceful streams at the building? Why aren't they extinguishing anything? Why are the majority of them standing by—doing nothing?

Advanced Drama clusters together, muttering questions and getting no answers. The red ball caps whisper, point at the building, shuffle their feet. Liz tugs at her bottom lip, worriedly muttering, "Oh, dear." Kiki wears her signature scowl. And Cass and Dylan appear at the same time, stepping into place beside me.

Cass even sleeps in vintage—or as close to vintage as possible. I already know that, but it's a source of amusement for everyone else. Tonight, her fuzzy pants are covered in a pattern featuring forties-era pinup girls in boy shorts, long legs, high heels.

Once everyone stops talking about Cass's sleepwear, the group falls serious again. The entire parking lot starts to take on the feel of a hospital waiting room crammed full of the anxious family members of a patient in surgery.

We fidget. After what seems like an eternity, the fire chief pulls his helmet from his head and waves the crowd closer.

We rush toward him, like fans at a concert all vying to be the first to touch him. He's got something we all crave—the answers: "How bad is it?" "What happened?" "Is it all gone?"

Because of my lousy shoe choice, I'm slower than the rest—at this point, my feet are practically numb, they're so cold. I get pushed toward the back. The fire chief's already speaking by the time I get to him. "Lightning," he's saying. But his voice is muffled. I can't make out the rest. And I can't see him at all.

Others begin to shout, "Speak up! We can't hear you!"

He grabs a megaphone from the truck and begins again as I push my way closer.

"Lightning hit the auditorium directly."

I look for Mom. It's easy to pinpoint her stark-white hair in the crowd. And even though I'm staring at her back, I can tell from the curve of her shoulders that she's dropped her face into her hands.

"Now, the strike was strong in intensity but relatively short in duration. It didn't start a fire. Its effect was more like an explosion."

"How could—" I'm not even sure I've said it out loud until every face in the crowd turns toward me. "How could there be a lightning strike when there was no rain? No storm?"

"Good question," a bathrobe-clad science instructor praises in his best third-period Intro to Earth Science voice. "There is such a thing as a dry thunderstorm." His voice gains strength, as if to indicate we should all be taking notes. "Precipitation evaporates before it hits the ground—"

"But we're the completely wrong climate here in Verona," another answers. "A dry thunderstorm occurs in the desert."

"Rogue strike," the firefighter says as a way to end the debate.

A flurry of questions flaps its wings all around me: "Electrical system?" "Rest of the building?" "School tomorrow?"

But my mind is stuck on the lightning—the wrong climate for dry storms.

"Now, the lightning," the firefighter goes on, "came straight through the ceiling, hit the stage. Knocked a nice-sized hole in it. Lots of smoke, no fire, like I said. We're doing a building check, but the way it looks right now, I see no reason why you can't hold classes tomorrow. Especially since the auditorium's the only area hit. You still have electricity. But the auditorium will definitely be off-limits."

My eyes turn toward the sky.

I shiver as the pieces begin to slide into place. We're in the wrong section of the country—too far south—to witness the aurora borealis. That's what Bertie told Mom the night Nick and Emma died. The sky has power over us—the power to change the course of events. Bertie said that, too. And now we find out we're in the wrong place for a dry thunderstorm.

Everyone else accepts it, breathing relieved sighs. The crowd breaks apart. Crisis averted. They simply peel off their worry, like dirty clothes to be tossed aside. Car engines crank to life and begin to leave the lot.

But the lightning was no freak accident. The sky is working its magic. Just like Bertie said it would. I was pushed into bed, into my dream, and hauled out of bed, then forced toward my window. I was supposed to see that last scene on the stage as it truly was, in graphic detail. I was supposed to see that lightning, too.

Connect the dots, Quin. The voice sounds like it's my own and coming from outside my head, all at the same time. *Connect the dots. . . .*

thirty-two

I've got to get to that auditorium. See it for myself.

But I'm not the only one who feels that way. The entire student body shows up early; the parking lot's so crammed, I have to circle it three times looking for a space. Cass is on my heels as we race inside, into the building that smells like a rained-on campfire, trying to wiggle through the crowded hallways.

The biggest crowd of all is congregated in front of the auditorium doors, which have been roped off by yellow Caution tape.

I'm not sure what to expect—that the entire auditorium will look like the bottom of a grill, maybe, with its gray charcoal smoldering. When I stick my head through the doorway, though, the seating is perfect. The walls are fine.

The only visible damage is to the front of the theater, where a giant, gaping crater has appeared in the center of the stage, leaving splintered boards to stick out at crazy angles. The damage also makes the stage seem smaller somehow, more fragile—it looks like a bowl with toothpicks sticking out.

The spotlight still apparently works, though. It shoots light straight down from the ceiling.

Nearby voices begin to bark instructions. A rattle fills the air. I lean into the auditorium, my side pushing against the Caution tape. Contractors in hard hats and reflective vests are on the roof—visible because of the hole in the ceiling. They drape a tarp over the hole, and the spotlight dies.

Of course it does. It's not a spotlight at all, but the sun, streaming through the hole the lightning created.

That lightning struck the stage like it was the bull's-eye in a target practice.

Everyone's in their seat in Advanced Drama a good two minutes before the bell. We lean forward. We don't blink. We stare at Mom, anxious to hear what she's got to say.

But she doesn't move after the bell announces the start of class. Mom's seated at her desk, under her "The Play's the Thing" banner, staring out her window. Exhaustion and the harsh sun make her look every last one of her years.

Unable to stand it any longer, Toby blurts, "Is there any

way we can still do the show?"

"Obviously not," Kiki says. "Didn't you see the way the fire department has the auditorium roped off?"

"Well, yeah, *now* it's roped off," Toby argues. "But if they put the tarps up and there's nothing wrong with the electrical system—is there a way to do it? We're all sitting here right now. It's not dangerous to be in the building. Why not take the ropes down, let us come in and do the musical?"

"It really would be a shame for all that work to go to waste," Liz says with a shake of her head. But she says it in the same way that a seven-year-old might feign sadness on learning they were allergic to vegetables. "I was so looking forward to seeing everyone in the audience wearing their vintage clothes. Still, you know, we probably would have gotten *far* more participation in the vintage clothes idea if it had been advertised on radio." She shoots me a look. "But it would have been fun just the same. Everyone would have enjoyed that, I think."

I practically need ropes to tie my eyes down, the urge to roll them is so strong.

Still, Mom stares through the window. Did she even hear us?

The clock ticks. The red ball caps shuffle their feet.

"Ms. Drewery?" Liz tries.

Mom finally pulls her eyes away from the window.

"We're going to have to cancel? Right?" Liz asks. "We won't be penalized for that, will we? We wouldn't get bad grades for the senior project because we won't be performing?"

"It's not our fault," Kiki says, palms stretched out innocently. She smiles like a cat with a canary in her gut.

Mom sighs heavily and stares at her hands as she flips a pen in her fingers, over and over again.

"I still think we can do it. I got the sign fixed," Toby insists, at the same moment he raises his hand. The other two red ball caps shake their heads at him as he says, "Come on! We just need one night."

"We can't touch anything in the auditorium," Mom finally mutters.

Every head in the room turns toward her as she goes on, "Not before the insurance adjuster gets there. Then it has to be repaired—even though the damage was isolated, it's still a bigger job than you're assuming it is. The gym is too small. And the cafeteria—that's out of the question. Which means we have nowhere to perform our musical."

We all hold our breath. Here it comes—the time to wave the white flag, throw in the towel, give up the ghost—and any other tried-and-true cliché that says the same thing: *defeat*.

Mom's words come out in a disjointed manner. "Too little too late." "Tried valiantly."

But as she talks, my mind is spinning, faster even than those records Cass has for sale on consignment in Duds. The lightning bolt destroyed our stage. Strategically. Only one theater remains in the entire town of Verona.

"Let's do it in the Avery," I blurt before I can stop myself.

The class turns their surprised stares at me. But I really only feel two of them: Cass's and Dylan's.

"You can't be serious," one of the red caps moans. "The Avery? We might as well do it in the parking lot. Or the city dump."

"Quin's right," Cass chimes in. "We should do it in the Avery."

She turns to offer me a thank-you grin laced with all the secrets she thinks she's been keeping from me. She wants back in. To be transformed one more time. To feel as she does when she and Dylan are standing beside each other on the stage.

But there's so much more at stake here.

We can't shut this play down. We have to perform it. It has to be on the stage of the Avery. I have no idea how. Not with the rust-scabs on the doors and Kiki, who was unwelcome before, and the sparks that no one else on the square has seen—not Vanessa or the Fergusons or even Mom. What will the rest of the class see when they arrive at the Avery's door? Dust and a toppled set and broken glass? Is that all? I'm terrified of what I've just suggested—and at the same time, completely sure it's right. The skies are insisting on it.

"The Avery," Mom repeats. She wiggles her jaw back and forth, thinking. "I have to make a few calls. I'll see what I can do."

thirty-three

We hear nothing the rest of the day. There's no word—
nor am I even sure how word would come to us. Or
what Mom's finding out. Or who she's calling.

Until the intercom buzzes.

My entire sixth-period English class turns their heads
toward the old black box poised over the chalkboard. It's happening in every classroom, I think. Every set of eyes turning
toward the old intercom boxes. A buzzing intercom all on its
own is usually pretty good at stealing a student body's attention, but today, after the lightning strike, everyone's been
saying: "Hey! Aren't you in drama? What about the musical?"
Or "Tough break." Or "Aren't you lucky?"

It's been on everyone's lips all day. Rumors have spread.
Wrong info and "I heards" and flat-out untruths have caught

on—a different version after each class.

Talk about drama.

Now everyone's turning their curious faces toward the intercom, wondering if this is it—the official word. It has to be, doesn't it? The school day's quickly rolling to a close.

"If I could have your attention, please. . . ." It's not the principal's voice that crackles through the intercom—it's Mom's.

"No need to dwell on the obvious," she announces. "We all know the Verona High auditorium was struck by lightning last night. What you don't know is that Advanced Drama is determined not to let it keep us from bringing you our production of *Anything Goes*. We mean to continue with our commitment to bringing attention to—and raising money for—the revival of the Avery Theater.

"One of my students has smartly suggested that we transfer tonight's show to the stage of the Avery. I have met today with two architects—parents of students here at our school—and the city building inspector, who's also a proud Verona High parent. They unanimously agreed that while it's looking worse for the wear, the Avery is, in fact, structurally sound. It poses no danger to the cast or audience. So the show will go on. At the Avery Theater, seven p.m."

Around me, the class erupts into mumbles of "You've got to be kidding" and "How's that possible"—so much so that I almost miss Mom's final message. "And, per instructions from the costume department, the audience is to show up in their finest vintage attire—whatever 'vintage' happens to mean to them. Cast members, listen up: Be at the theater no later than five thirty. Be prompt—and bring your best *Anything Goes* attitude."

My phone blows up the second the final bell rings. A flurry of texts pours in from everyone in Advanced Drama. And, surprisingly enough, the kids in choir. The art kids. And a couple of guys from the soccer team. All of them wanting to know what Mom's thinking.

Several of them want to know what *I'm* thinking. Because everyone in drama's blabbed that the Avery idea's mine. They're all acting like I've officially lost it. Their collective reaction feels even stronger to me than the way the town had once responded to poor, crazy Bertie.

When I don't answer right away, the sender shoots another text, quickly followed by another. I walk down to the parking lot with my nose in my screen. It stays there as Cass drives us to the square.

"What're you telling everyone?" she asks.

I sigh, lowering the phone into my lap. I know this is her own way of sending a text.

"I haven't replied yet," I admit.

"To anyone?"

"Nope."

"But when you do, though. What'll you say?"

"I don't know."

"I mean—everybody in drama. We kind of need to know what we're doing here. What'll we do for costumes? They were in the auditorium. They're full of smoke now, and we're not allowed on the stage to get them, anyway. Quin? What're we supposed to wear?"

"Dunno."

"The set?"

"Dunno."

"Quin! The Avery was your idea!"

"I just—"

As she pulls to a stop in front of Potions, her eyes are pleading. But I have no idea what to say. I have no way to calm her fears. We've never talked about any of this out loud—not the Avery. Not the way she looked inside. Not the way Dylan spoke. Not about the bond that's been growing between them.

I shrug. "I'll see you in a couple of hours."

"Quin!" she shouts over the putter of her VW engine.

I pretend not to hear as I unlock the door to Potions and race upstairs. So far, this afternoon, the Avery has cooperated with my wild idea. There's no rust on the door—at least, it let the inspectors and Mom inside. What if I mess up this whole thing? What if the Avery's listening, and I suddenly say the wrong thing? What if everything that's happening—this whole crazy, wild story—has brakes, like a train, and it could all come to a sudden, screaming stop right here?

I toss my backpack on my bed, more panicked than I've

ever been. I could actually hyperventilate—or have a stroke. *What am I going to do now?*

I can hear the door swing. Mom's home.

And I need answers.

Even as she steps into my room, I'm reaching into my backpack. I need Bertie's journal. Her map. There has to be something—just one answer—in there somewhere. Something I missed the last time I looked at it.

Maybe it would help make Mom remember something.

Mom flops down on my bed. "What a day," she sighs. "Quin, what in the world are we about to do?"

I tug out Bertie's journal, accidentally knocking out a yellowing envelope along with it. The one I found in George's apartment. I never did open it—in fact, I'd forgotten I dropped it in my backpack in the first place.

"It's for you," I say, holding it out to her. "Trouble" is scrawled across the aged front, in a man's cursive writing.

"No one's called me that in— Where'd you get this?"

"The Avery," I say.

"You were inside? How?"

"I, well— A skeleton key lock's easy to pick and—George's apartment—upstairs," I babble. I don't care that I'm admitting it. In that instant, it doesn't seem like dangerous territory anymore, not with Mom—not like talking about the Avery's magic with Cass felt dangerous a moment before.

"There's money in here," Mom says, tearing it open. And

a letter—on similarly yellow paper. I'm already looking over her shoulder as she gently spreads it open:

Little Trouble,

You have always been my other girl. The one who loved my theater as much as I did. I watched you grow, and I missed having you around sticking your nose where it didn't belong. I'm giving you my precious Avery. You're the one who'll know what to do with it. After all, you're the one who said you'd sell magic hats when you were grown. Hats that transformed the people wearing them. What is that, other than a costume? You, I'm certain, will be my helper even after I'm gone. The one who will ensure the magic of the theater will continue on.

I'm also sending along Emma's college money. We saved it—bit by bit, in an old glass jar, always with the best of intentions, dreaming of the chance she would get to spend it. She never got to use it. You should have it.

I know you've always hated being little. I know you've never heard that word as I did—as a term of endearment. But Little Trouble, there are no small parts. And in my story,

*your part is the least small of them all. I
believe in you, as much as I believed in my
own Emma, and as I always believed in the
magic of the theater.*

—George

She scrambles to get back inside the envelope. "The deed,"
Mom says, astounded. "The *deed*? And three thousand dol-
lars," she continues, quickly counting it. "Doesn't sound like
much now, but back then, it was huge. I'm sure it took forever
to save that much. Emma had a scholarship, but she would
have needed to buy books and clothes, and she'd have needed
money to travel back and forth to visit her dad. I can't believe
this. I own it?"

"There's something else inside, Mom."

When she tugs the envelope back open, the item we see
inside brings instant relief; the universe has come full circle.
It's a sign that, as Mom might say, all's well that ends well.
The cloth flower. The one I found on the balcony. The one
she dropped the night of the accident. How it got in the envelope is the stuff of mystery, but I'm not questioning it. No
more than I'd ever question any good turn of fortune.

The moment Mom touches the flower, the front of the
Avery explodes. A shower of sparks flies across the entire square.
The night sky returns. The marquee comes to life, proclaiming

in black letters and brilliant white light, ANYTHING GOES! Beneath the glow of nearby streetlights, graffiti disappears. Hedges are green. The grass is lush. The awning over the front walk blows in the breeze—instantly repaired.

Mom trembles, pointing. "I can't— Did you see—?"

"Of course I did," I say.

She races outside; I'm on her heels, journal in hand.

Halfway across the square, Bertie's journal flops open. I watch as every last one of her handwritten words flies from the pages, straight up into the air. They hover, then slowly begin to blink over the patch of grass outside the Avery. Her words are fireflies, blinking and swarming feverishly.

I take a few steps down the front walk, marveling at the sight of Bertie's words. Just as quickly as they all fanned out, they congregate again, forming a ribbon that zips straight back to Bertie's pages.

I slam the journal shut, hug it to my chest. I don't know what this means yet, but I glance up and down the square, half expecting Bertie to emerge. She doesn't, though—and Mom's already stepping through the entrance, which has been left wide open, like an invitation. I'm shaky, but race to catch up with her.

Inside, the lobby is welcoming. The concession stand is full. The smell of butter wafts. As if freshly dusted, the chandeliers sparkle. On the opposite side of the large double doors, the rows of seats are plush. The velvet curtains have been drawn open, revealing a stage with a gleaming wooden floor. The *Anything Goes* set is artistic—and complete—and unbroken.

Mom stands in the center aisle, mesmerized. I pass her, pointing to the rack on the side of the stage and shouting, "The costumes! Look! They're here!"

"And the piano," I go on, pointing toward the pit. "It looks new. This whole place is perfect."

"But I swear it wasn't just earlier today," Mom says tearfully. "When I was here with the inspectors."

Overwhelmed and confused, we turn toward each other and laugh.

Relaxing my grip on Bertie's journal, I glance down to find that my name is in dark letters on the cover—now it's "Alberta" that's barely visible under "Quin."

Standing on the stage, I open it and begin to read.

The words in her journal now make perfect sense. They've rearranged themselves outside and no longer sound at all like the rantings of a madwoman. I see Dahlia in these pages. I feel her heartbreak—which Bertie witnessed and described after Emma died. I see a little girl who thought she broke her promises. I see, too, that Dahlia broke nothing. She saved it, all of it—this journal and the map and me. And here we are, nesting dolls a step apart, here for the same purpose. There's no longer a need for a key.

I flip to the back, where my own words fill the last pages. Now I understand exactly what I have to do.

thirty-four

But just because I suddenly know what I need to do doesn't mean I'm not terrified. It's like I've realized that in order to pull this whole thing off, I'm going to have to jump from a cliff, leap across a canyon, and safely land on the other side— while dragging the entire class with me.

When the first few Advanced Drama nobodies arrive, their footsteps clicking loudly through the theater, I step to the edge of the stage and shade my eyes with my hand. The footlights seem especially harsh—every bit as harsh as my fear.

I step out of the glare to find Kiki and Liz standing in the center aisle waving me over.

Yes. Kiki's here, and the Avery's still lit up and looking new. This is the right time. This is the moment it all comes together.

The moment that Bertie foretold all those years ago. It's happening, it's happening. . . .

"This was inside all along? Did you have any idea when you suggested we use the Avery?" Liz asks.

"How could this be? It doesn't even smell old," Kiki chimes in. "It used to—" But she stops short of admitting she was here, interrupting Cass and Dylan's private practice.

"How can the neon sign outside still be working after all this time?" Liz asks. "Wasn't it broken?"

"Yeah!" Toby shouts as he bursts into the theater. "The electric's on! And I've got the screen." He holds up a finger. "It's in my truck. Wait just a second."

I remind Liz she has a job to do, pointing at the costume rack on the stage.

The first dress on the rack is perfect for Kiki. The next garment—a suit—works fine for Toby. He grabs it, then quickly rushes to attach his enormous screen to the rigging— with the help of the other two red ball caps, who have arrived as well.

The rest of the class trickles in slowly. And each time a new face shows up, it's washed in shock, confusion, even bewilderment—but never disbelief. How can you not believe something that's right in front of you? Especially when everyone else sees the same thing you do?

Up on the stage, Liz's eyes sparkle joyfully. Each time she

removes one costume, another slides to the front of the rack—and it's perfect for the next person in line. "Everything's the right size," she keeps muttering. "How's that possible?" Then giggles. "Isn't it wonderful?"

Toby keeps calling me over, asking for feedback on his hopeless screen. "Is it straight?" he asks. "Are you sure?"

Between nods, I peek through a tiny gap in the middle of the now-drawn curtains. "Quiet! Everyone's coming," I hiss over my shoulder.

I wave Liz over to take a look, too. They're all in vintage. For the most part, they appear to have pulled out a few old pieces from the backs of their own closets—or their parents' closets. Some of the parents are even in the letter jackets they wore years ago to parade through the halls of Verona High. Those faces from the school fire are all here—in their vintage garb, they all look just as young as they had the night of the lightning strike—and I feel it again: that sense that the story bubbling around us is ours, all together. Not just mine. Or Mom's. Or Cass's. It belongs to those who are flipping down their seats, settling in to watch the show, every bit as much as it belongs to those of us who are about to perform it. *Now*, I think, *if I can just present it in a way that makes them feel that, too.*

The crowd murmurs, pointing at the gilded embellishments, the sparkling chandeliers, the floral carpet. The same cluster of choir kids who crashed our rotten first rehearsal are all checking their tickets—the same tickets they surely bought weeks ago, when the announcement of our production was first made. They're pointing at seats, their ticket stubs matching up with the rows in the Avery—as though it were somehow predestined all along that this was where our performance would take place.

With no wisecracks—and too stunned even to think about getting out their phones—they settle into their plush seats. Eyeing each other. Shrugging. Shaking their heads.

When Cass arrives, her eyes are the widest of all. The Avery has never done this before, not to this extent—the lights, the perfect interior.

The dress now at the front of the costume rack is blue. A perfect match for the familiar pillbox hat with mesh resting on the top shelf, beside the mirror.

Cass's hand shakes as she reaches for the hat. Stepping before the mirror, she secures it to the top of her head. A shower of sparks tumbles down the side of her face, scrubbing her birthmark away.

"Cass," Liz gasps.

Which draws the attention of the rest of the class. Suddenly, they're all talking, pointing. One races to pull the last person from the dressing room. But this attention doesn't sting. It tickles Cass into a round of laughter.

Dylan steps into view, reaching through the students who have clustered around Cass to retrieve the next garment on the rack: Nick's jacket. The moment he slides into it, another puff of sparks flies from his shoulders.

"Should I warm up the piano?" Dylan asks me with no struggle or stutter or hiccup.

"Not yet," I say. "I'm going to need you onstage. I'm changing things around."

But hardly anyone hears me. Everyone's still marveling at what's happened to Dylan. "He— How?" they all ask.

I catch Cass's eye—she's waiting for my response. My shock, my hurt, even, that this secret of hers is in the open. I smile—and in that smile, I say, *It's okay, Cass. It makes me so happy to see you this way.* It all makes me happy—the new face she wears, the way it makes her feel, even Dylan. What's happening between her and Dylan makes me happy, too—no jealousy about it.

How can I be jealous when they obviously opened this thing up? Together, with their first impromptu performace, they unlocked the Avery. They unleashed that first burst of sparks and let me see the old theater in a new way. Dropped this new scene right into my lap.

Always before, I've taken others' stories and made them into something I could use—all those novels in my room becoming furniture. Now it's up to me to take pieces of others' stories—Bertie's and Mom's and Emma's and even Cass's—and string them into a story of my own. But can I? I never have before. Not out loud. Not like this. I start to sweat.

Noises trickling through the curtain from the audience sound louder than before—every murmur punches my eardrum.

And suddenly, I'm reliving the joy that found me as I scribbled new passages in the back of Bertie's journal at the same time I'm remembering Bertie's words: *This is a once-in-forever love that has the power to change the world around it.*

This was Alberta's prediction for me all along—why my name was on her journal. My love of words—but is it enough? Can I pull off what I'm imagining?

Cass must read all that in my face, because I swear, when she smiles back at me, I see her saying, *You can. You have that kind of power.*

Her smile fades as the lights dim.

"Who did that? Is the curtain about to come up?" Kiki asks. "You haven't told us what we're doing. If it's not what we practiced . . ."

Darkness explodes. The entire cast is backing up, eyes glowing like animals looking for a place to hide. Let's face it—we've never been good. We've had a few decent moments in rehearsal, sure. But any time we've even dared to think we were getting somewhere, the outside world—a radio station interview, a few comments under a YouTube video—would haul us right back into reality. For the most part, we've all been afraid of becoming an online laughingstock.

The curtains are starting to slide open.

It's showtime.

I step to the center of the stage, wearing a red-and-white seersucker dress. The same dress I saw on Bertie the first time we met face-to-face on the square. "Welcome to the Avery Theater," I announce. "I'm Quin Drewery, the director—and"—I take a deep lungful of air—"the writer—of tonight's production. You all arrived tonight expecting to see the Advanced Drama class perform the original *Anything Goes*. But tonight we're going to be sharing another story, one that has been waiting a long time to be told.

"Our production is also called *Anything Goes*. But it's a story whose beginning is rooted in truth. In the past—in *our* past. What's past is prologue, as the Bard said. So we invite you to come with us as we relive the final tragedy that played out right here on this stage. A tragedy not of the page but, as I said, of real life."

I take a deep breath. Open Bertie's journal as if to read from it. "It's June 1947," I announce. When I sweep my arm out to the side, a shower of sparks explodes; in their wake, the square appears. The old square, the bustling square. Right there on the stage. All of it—the cars, the streetlights. On one end of the square, the Avery looks new. The class takes up the roles of the Verona residents of 1947, all of them racing from one store to the next, calling happily to one another.

The auditorium fills with gasps.

"This story involves a real-life Romeo and Juliet," I

announce. When I point, Cass and Dylan emerge, both of them dressed as Emma and Nick.

Those scenes that we'd put together in rehearsal that had never seemed to have much of a place fit perfectly now. I hadn't been revising the boy-wants-girl story in the script as much as trying to find a way to write down the love story I'd been watching play out between Emma and Nick. Cass realizes it, too, falling right into the dialogue I've already penned and that she's already memorized. Dylan follows suit.

Another surprised murmur ripples through the theater. Her birthmark. His stutter. Both gone.

I take up the role of Bertie as narrator, pointing at the skies, saying, "This is a tale of star-crossed lovers. Ill-fated. But I know there's more to it. I know about the magic that exists in the world. If only you'll let yourself see it."

A wild yellow streak bursts in the air above Cass. It snakes along the ceiling of the theater, swirling and cascading over the audience.

As their characters begin to fall in love, an electric-green light shoots above Dylan, dancing alongside Cass's yellow streaks.

"These are the same colors that rose from the horizon on that tragic night in 1947," I continue in my storytelling voice. "The same colors I always knew could not be the aurora borealis. Verona's in the wrong place, after all—too far south. Tonight, though, we're all in the right place to bring them back."

As we move deeper into the first act, the players lose any last semblance of clumsiness. They're no longer stiff or robotic. Cass's and Dylan's lights continue to curl about the air, and that somehow changes what the entire class thinks they're capable of. They're suddenly all infused with confidence, some of them even going so far as to exhibit a newly acquired swagger.

When I'm not on the stage myself, I hiss directions at my classmates, giving them the gist of the next scene, telling them what their motivation is before pushing them back out to perform. The colors of the overhead light show deepen, intensify as the story moves forward—the color of a first crush becomes the color of a first kiss becomes the color of not wanting to ever let go.

The cast's improvised words are spot-on, filled with just the right sprinkles of emotion. As though in answer, lights begin to rise from them: purples and pinks and blues, joining together in the space above our heads to complete the display.

The audience responds, giggling at Emma's clumsiness. Sighing as Emma and Nick grow closer. Clucking their tongues in disapproval when George tries to tear them apart. Shaking their heads at little Trouble and her meddlesome ways. Cocking their heads to the side, feeling sorry for Bertie.

The cast begins to feed off the audience—every response encourages them, makes them better than they were just a moment before.

Mom was right—they're rising to the occasion.

And she knows it. When I glance her way backstage, she's smiling. Tears glitter behind her glasses.

When the curtains fall on the first act, I'm anxious to see what the response is. I peek through the gap in the red velvet; the audience is visibly moved. The powerful last scene—the death of the two star-crossed lovers—has them dabbing the corners of their eyes. Shaking their heads. Murmuring to the person seated at their side. *I've got them,* I think. *They see what I see. Feel what I feel. We're doing it.*

As Act II opens, I return to the stage, wearing a pair of khaki shorts and a white T-shirt, along with my cat's-eye glasses. "Now, we leave the past behind," I insist. The set responds, following my instruction. The bustling square of 1947 turns into the empty, dilapidated square of today.

The audience falls into stunned silence.

Behind me, the entire class emerges, all of them in their normal daily clothes—red ball caps, jeans, Cass's vintage polyester maxidress, Dylan's black T-shirt and skeleton key necklace.

"How do you uncross stars?" I ask. Behind me, Toby lets out a yelp of triumph as his screen takes flight, soaring up into the air. The screen fades, as do the wires of the Christmas lights, replaced by a ceiling full of twinkling stars.

"How do you rewrite history?" I ask. "How do you fix something as tragic as Nick and Emma's story?"

I let my question hang beneath the aurora borealis swirls and the stars.

"You don't," I say simply. "You don't rewrite history. You don't revise the past." I couldn't—not even when I was crying out to Emma from the balcony, yelling at her to watch out before she took that final tumble. She couldn't hear me, no matter how loud I screamed. "You don't bring Nick and Emma back. You can't change what's already taken place.

"The past isn't just written," I go on. "It's etched. Bertie's is. The Avery's is. You don't erase that. But if you keep moving, keep pushing the story forward, adding brighter sentences— then it isn't a tragedy anymore. The dark time becomes a sad scene in the middle of a tale of triumph. A sour note that can lead to a richer, more beautiful chord."

I point, making a piano appear in the middle of the stage. Cass and Dylan sit at the bench. Dylan starts with a few introductory chords; Cass hums. Slowly, the words to the songs we've learned for *Anything Goes* begin to swell.

And suddenly, the entire cast is involved in a medley, dancing and belting the lyrics to "It's De-Lovely" and "I Get a Kick Out of You." Kiki's front and center now, hitting the arm of the red ball cap beside her, egging him on, pushing him forward. *Come on, come on, this is fantastic. Keep up. Keep going.*

As they perform, the set begins to reinvent itself, to depict the Verona town square as it could still be. Lights return. The

Avery's windows are no longer cracked. Signs appear. The sounds of car engines and voices and laughter spill out from all directions.

The square in the center of the stage is vibrant. Bustling.

Of course it is. Anything you imagine is real here. That's truly the magic of the theater.

The cast falls quiet as Dylan's piano leads Cass into a solo performance of "You'd Be So Easy to Love."

Cass and Dylan are both themselves and unlike themselves at that moment; on the stage, they're characters we've all seen or befriended in real life. Characters we've all been. At that moment, the members of the audience are right there, with Cass, falling in love for the first time all over again. Whatever separated them from that old love no longer exists. And for those who haven't fallen yet, whatever obstacle has ever stood in their way is gone. Just as Cass's birthmark is gone, as Dylan's stutter is gone. At that moment, first love is a present tense, with nothing in the way of a happy ending.

Star-crossed lovers uncrossed.

The aurora borealis colors begin to shift in the space above our heads. The previously stationary streaks of color are moving, like lines being drawn by an invisible pen, bouncing from one person to another. Bouncing between the audience and the players. Tying us together. Connecting us—like dots—to create a bigger picture. The past and the present, who we are and who we wish we were coming together on the stage. All that's needed to witness the magic is just a spark of belief.

From somewhere deep in the background, a drumbeat begins to thump out a syncopated rhythm. But I know that's not a drum at all. The Avery's heart is beating. The Avery, that old woman, is alive. And young again. The Avery has risen from the dead.

We join together for one more rousing number—"Anything Goes." And at that moment, it's true. Now that the town has seen it, the soul of the theater alive and well, anything can happen. As the play winds down, everyone inside the walls of the Avery knows that Verona is at the beginning of a new act of its own.

Once the final note stops echoing, the audience is on their feet. Applause erupts.

Curtain calls. Whistles. Bravos.

"Go," Mom says. "Take your bows. You deserve them."

I grab her hand and haul her—the new owner of the Avery—out with us.

She glances out into the auditorium, a young woman coming face-to-face with her old love again. And more—her eyes sparkle in the stage lights as she stands in the midst of sad, sour endings that now can be bumps in the road.

"See? You kept your promise," I tell her as we all line up at the edge of the stage.

She bows with the rest of the class—all of us drenched in sweat, but ecstatic.

Epilogue

Needless to say, every one of us got an A on our senior project.

Ever since our night in the Avery, Advanced Drama has been treated as far more than just the plain old Grays and Navy Blues in the crayon box. We've become Electric Lime, Laser Lemon, Razzmatazz. Next year when Jenny's back, the drama class is going to have (as Mom puts it) a deuce of a time figuring out how to live up to the bar we've raised.

Finally—Advanced Drama has made its mark.

Most days the construction crew Mom hired is out in front of the Avery, beneath an ever-present rainbow that appeared the day after our show and has never faded, sticking to the sky through rain or shine. They scrub away graffiti, fix windows. Spruce up the marquee. Replace the bulbs in the neon sign.

Work themselves to nubs because everyone in town sees the possibility of what the old theater can be.

The square's getting new visitors—contractors and architects studying the old buildings for renovation. Two of them have sold. Rosarita's has a permanent sign.

Cass and Dylan still go to work after school, but most days they leave together. Walk across the square hand in hand. A couple of times I catch them in the alley behind the Avery, Cass with her arms around Dylan's neck, their faces pressed together. They remind me, at those times, of the cover I once saw on Emma's *Love Fiction Monthly*. A sight that puts a dip in my stomach—either makes me start fantasizing about my own future love story or inspires me, sends me racing to open a new file on my computer. Start typing away.

When Saturday weather cooperates, Cass and Dylan can even be found on the curb outside of Ferguson's, Dylan strumming his guitar while Cass sings musical standards—often drawing a small crowd from the increasing square traffic. But an audience never sends them scattering off. They're no longer the best musicians no one has ever heard perform.

As for me, I've already gotten the college acceptance letter I realized I really wanted—to a school here in state. Mom gave me Emma's college money. "It's like George knew you'd be part of it all," Mom said. "A gift for you and a gift for me in his envelope. After that production, nobody deserves his money more than you do." I figure George's scholarship fund will go further if I'm not paying out-of-state tuition.

Besides, I don't want to be too far from Mom. And the Avery.

I suppose we all found love through the Avery—the theater brought Cass and Dylan together, but it also made them take their places center stage. Made them walk into the spotlight. And Mom—she didn't just inherit an old building. She got to revisit her past—renew old passions, dust off old dreams. It's never too late, after all.

I finally fessed up to my own dreams (as Mom also often phrases it). Nothing about my own story is a confused connect-the-dots pattern anymore. I know exactly who I am—where I fit in and what I want. After what happened in the Avery, there's no way I'll ever be shoving stories into old hatboxes. I'm not a closet scribbler anymore.

Now when I dream, I'm no longer in the audience, staring up at a screen. I'm still in the Avery—that hasn't changed— but I'm directing my own original play. Sometimes the play is my college thesis. Sometimes it's my hundredth play.

Always, though, applause is strong enough to make the walls tremble.

Because the space between what is and what could be— isn't that the most magical place of all?

Acknowledgments

As the credits roll on this project, I want to thank the crew at HarperCollins, with special thanks, yet again, to my editor, Karen Chaplin. I also want to thank my always-supportive agent, Deborah Warren. Warmest gratitude to Team Schindler (my sounding board, first reader, and loudest and most enthusiastic cheering section), and to my readers, especially those devoted book junkies and bloggers who have been with me since the beginning. I'm also grateful, this time, for my Midwestern roots, for small towns with old-fashioned squares much like the fictionalized square of Verona. For weekends spent watching vintage movies on the screens of antique theaters that became the inspiration for the Avery. . . .